REDWING

HOLLY BENNETT

ORCA BOOK PUBLISHERS

Library and Archives Canada Cataloguing in Publication

Bennett, Holly, 1957-
Redwing / Holly Bennett.

Issued also in electronic formats.
ISBN 978-1-4598-0038-0

I. Title.
PS8603.E5595R43 2012   jc813'.6   C2012-902217-9

First published in the United States, 2012
Library of Congress Control Number: 2012937566

Summary: Rowan, a young musician whose entire family has died from the plague,
forms an uneasy alliance with a young man who possesses peculiar powers.

*Orca Book Publishers is dedicated to preserving the environment and has printed
this book on paper certified by the Forest Stewardship Council ®.*

Orca Book Publishers gratefully acknowledges the support for its publishing
programs provided by the following agencies: the Government of Canada through
the Canada Book Fund and the Canada Council for the Arts, and the Province of British
Columbia through the BC Arts Council and the Book Publishing Tax Credit.

Cover artwork by Juliana Kolesova
Cover design by Teresa Bubela
Author photo by Mark Burstyn

ORCA BOOK PUBLISHERS
PO Box 5626, Stn. B
Victoria, BC Canada
V8R 6S4

ORCA BOOK PUBLISHERS
PO Box 468
Custer, WA USA
98240-0468

www.orcabook.com
Printed and bound in Canada.

15 14 13 12 • 4 3 2 1

*Five novels, and I still haven't dedicated one to
my husband, John. It's well past time! From my first
tentative pages, he has supported me on this labor of love
that is writing. He chauffeurs me on wild-goose-chase
research jaunts, celebrates every new title and brags
about my books when I'm too shy to mention them.
Plus, his music seems to weave through all my novels—
especially this one. Thanks, my man:
I am lucky to have you.*

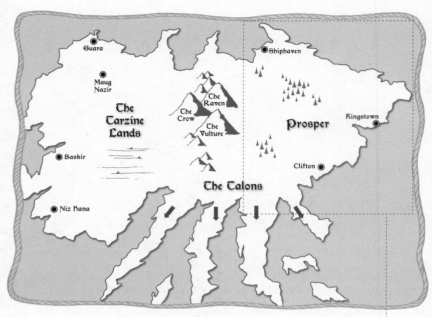

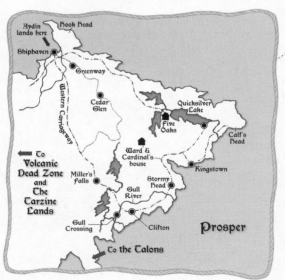

·ONE

The caravan was never intended for winter use. When the wind came up, whatever heat Rowan could coax from the smoky little stove seeped right through the canvas walls. He prayed for calm weather, and on bad nights like this he huddled shivering in a roll of blankets, listening to the canvas rustle and crack like a ship's sail. He never felt more alone than on these black, moaning nights. Sleep seemed impossible—until, at last, it took him by surprise, and he escaped into uneasy dreams.

Rowan!

He raised his head groggily. "What's wrong, Ettie?" His sister's voice had been sharp with alarm. Then he remembered. Not Ettie—just a dream. He slumped back into his mattress, hoping that sleep would reclaim him before the memories did.

Rowan!

Rowan sat up this time. The voice seemed so clear. Then he leaped to his feet.

The caravan floor was on fire. The sensations hit him all at once: the smell of acrid smoke, the jumpy, crazy light of flames, an icy blast of wind, the noisy flap of canvas.

Ripping the blankets off his bunk, Rowan threw them over the blazing floorboards. The caravan went pitch-black. He beat at the flames through the thick covering, cursing as his hand hit the squat shape of the stove. That must be where the fire started, he realized. Usually the little bucket-shaped stove sat in a snug metal housing under the galley cooktop, but Rowan had moved it into the middle of the floor in an attempt to warm up his bed. He peeled the blanket back over the top of the stove and then tried to grab the stove handle to haul it away from the fire. He yelped as the hot handle bit into his palm and again as he smacked his head on the edge of his bunk while groping for some kind of padding for his hands. Finally he stripped off his own nightshirt and used it like a pot holder to drag the stove out the door and into the snowy night.

Back inside, the flames seemed to be out but Rowan still pounded every square inch of the blanket to be sure. Then he felt his way to the lamp by his bed, scraped the spark striker and lit it. He unclipped it from its rack and peered around.

The caravan was basically a long wagon with chest-high sides topped with a frame over which was stretched a canvas ceiling and walls. The canvas flaps could be rolled up and tied in fine weather to allow sunshine and fresh air inside. With a tiny galley at the front, a single drop-down bunk along each side and a larger platform bed at the back, the caravan was a cozy, comfortable travel home for a family of four—in the summer.

It didn't take long to find where the wind was coming from. A canvas fastener had ripped loose right above his sister's bunk, leaving a flapping breach open to the weather. A pile of wet snow lay clumped on the wooden sleeping ledge. Rowan grabbed the loose canvas flap and wrestled it back into position, then tried to think how to fix it. The childish part of him wanted to simply roll back up in his blankets and let the other side of the caravan fill with snow. But his blankets were scorched, and there was no one to deal with this but him, so he made his way through the cold caravan to the store box. He found a length of rope, fished again for the flap and found the broken fastener. There was, as he'd hoped, enough of a stub to tie on the rope as an extension. Then he lashed it around the cleat and tied it off. He'd try to neaten the repair in the morning.

He gathered up the smoldering blankets and threw them out the door. Maybe they were salvageable, but he wouldn't find out till morning. He scooped the snow from his sister's bunk onto the burnt floorboards, where it melted instantly. Still warm. How could he sleep, he wondered, with no way of being sure there wasn't a spark hidden in a crack, waiting to be coaxed into flame? He made one last trip, this time to the galley, where he kept the clean water. Half a bucket left. Rowan dumped a large puddle onto the floor and then padded on damp, freezing feet to a storage bin. He hauled out the two spare blankets and scrambled into his bunk.

I could have died, he thought, shaken at how easily he might have slept until it was too late. He was too exhausted and overwhelmed to push back the thought that slipped in next: *Better, maybe, if I had.*

THE NIGHT'S SNOW had nearly melted away when Rowan woke. The day was decent for traveling—overcast but mild, with a teasing hint in the air of the spring to come. It was actually pleasant to sit up front and drive the mules, and as he chewed on the end of bread he had saved from the day before, Rowan tried not to worry about how bony Dusty and Daisy looked. "You'll have a good feed soon, girls," he promised.

Funny how good things came from bad, he mused. His first discovery was that there hadn't been much fire damage to the floor after all. Mostly what had burned were his clothes from the day before, left in a heap when he changed for bed. Stupid to leave them so close to the stove. A stray spark blown by the wind gusting through the open flap was all it had taken to set them alight. His search for tools to repair the broken fastener had led him to a second, even better, discovery: a small lockbox tucked under the needles and yarn and fabric scraps in his mother's sewing kit. He didn't have the key, but he did have an ax, and soon he was fingering a stash of money—a few coins, mostly paper scrip—that must represent whatever his father was able to grab before their hasty flight from their home at Five Oaks. Two months on his own had already taught Rowan enough about costs to realize that it wasn't going to last him long. To keep it safe, he had divided the money up and hidden half in the caravan, half in the lining of his button box case. He intended to keep it for emergencies only—but a mule team on the edge of collapse *was* an emergency, and he had kept out enough for a few bales of hay and enough oats to see them through the last weeks of winter.

TWO·

Samik made his way down the gangplank and stumbled as the ground heaved under his feet. Raucous laughter erupted from the sailors behind him. "Lost your land legs in only a week? Maybe you'd best stay in your cabin where it's safe!" one gravelly voice teased.

Samik turned, fighting the feeling that he needed to sway to stay upright. How very odd, to be rolling over waves on dry land! He offered the burly, tattooed sailor a formal bow (despite the risk of pitching headfirst into the cobblestones) and a wry smile. "You'd like that, wouldn't you, Azir, having me with you forever? I'm touched that you'll miss me so much." More hoots of laughter, this time at Azir's expense.

"No, I must be off," Samik continued. "But I thank you for my safe passage. I'd like to compliment the comfort of the accommodations and quality of the food, but sadly…"

He gave an eloquent, rippling shrug and set off carefully down the quay, keeping K'waaf close beside him.

The dockside area of Shiphaven was not so different from Guara, the Tarzine port he'd sailed from: noisy, crowded, rough around the edges. The people were different though. Prosperian dress was awfully drab—so much brown and beige and black! Did they not know how to dye cloth? And it was strange to be surrounded by a foreign language. Samik's mother had taught him well, but the rough speech of the dock workers was a far cry from her cultured tongue.

Now what? he asked himself. "I must be off," he had announced grandly, but in truth he had no actual destination. "Head inland," his father had advised him. But where, and how?

First things first. Jago's men would not be on his heels— they might not even realize he had fled the country. Surely he had a few days, at least, to take his bearings and make a plan.

A room, a bath and a meal. That was a good plan. But he would make his way a little farther into town, away from the docks, even if the price of lodging was higher. If Jago's men did come later and ask around, he didn't want anyone to remember him.

THREE DAYS LATER, Samik was feeling much steadier, and not just on his legs. His ear was becoming attuned to the language, and he had found a comfortable room with a kindly widow amusingly named Missus Broadbeam.

While the landlord of the first lodging house he had tried had taken one look at K'waaf, muttered "no dogs" and hastily closed the door, Missus Broadbeam had fawned over the huge beast as though he were a baby. She had taken a shine to Samik too—her grandson, she said, had the same long white-blond hair, and that seemed to make Samik an honorary relative. So when she asked about his plans at breakfast on the third day, he decided to confide something of his plight.

"Oh, my dear!" Missus Broadbeam pressed her hand to her ample bosom and cast her eyes to heaven. "Oh, you poor lamb. All on your own, and with a price on your head? And your mother must be that worried about you!"

It was Missus Broadbeam who declared he must change his name. "Otherwise, you might just as well tell everyone you meet you're a Tarzine foreigner!" And so Aydin was born.

In fact, Missus Broadbeam was a fountain of good advice. She had asked Samik about his viol, and he confessed that he hoped to earn some money with his playing, since what he had come with would not last long. "Oh, that's grand. Musicians are very well regarded here," she enthused. "Would you do me a favor, dearie, and play me a little something? It would do my heart good."

But Samik—Aydin, now, and he'd best start getting used to it—hadn't played long before Missus Broadbeam scrunched up her face. "Now, no offense to your music, my dear, it's very lovely I'm sure," she said, "but you can't be pretending to be one of us and play that outlandish stuff. And once you're away from the port towns, you won't make much coin at it either. The country folk are not like us in Shiphaven, who are used to all sorts. They like what they know."

Missus Broadbeam had directed Samik to a shop where he could buy music for popular Prosperian tunes, and to a market where he might be able to find cheap passage inland with a farmer or merchant. She had even pressed a half-dallion into his hand when he said goodbye the next day. "A little off the rent, to help your travels," she said.

Riding in the back of a farm wagon was a bone-jarring experience, and Samik was grateful when, a good half-day later, the farmer pulled his mule to a halt and pointed down the road that branched off to the right. "There's a town that way. Greenway. 'Bout three miles."

Three miles. Samik didn't relish the hike, but at least he should reach the town before dark. He climbed out the back of the wagon, shouldered his pack and his viol, and started walking. He would find a place to stay the night and keep traveling in the morning.

THREE

Rowan clip-clopped the mules into the little town's market square and sized up his prospects. Fair to middling, he judged, especially for this time of year—busy enough to have plenty of customers, not so crowded that it would be hard for him to get noticed.

He found a spot for the caravan and climbed down to coax the girls backward into place. What was the name of this town, he wondered, annoyed that he had forgotten. Not that it mattered. Middleton, Waterford, Longview, Oak Ridge—they were all much the same, a string of nondescript settlements with unimaginative names. Cedar Glen—that was it.

The sound of a fiddle stopped him in his tracks. *Damn.* Rowan scanned the square again, searching for his competitor.

A tall boy, a little older than Rowan, stood in the gap between a wagon filled with chicken crates and a table of wizened root vegetables. A gust of wind lifted his long pale hair like a flag as he drew the bow across the strings of his instrument and then adjusted the tuning.

The dog that stood watchfully just behind the fiddler was the biggest Rowan had ever seen. Easily as tall as the shaggy little ponies they bred in the highlands, the wiry gray hound was clearly on guard.

Rowan considered. The next town was too far to reach in time for market; he'd have to hope for an inn that would let him play. That meant no food till nightfall, and then only if he was lucky.

There was an unwritten code for street performers: you don't impinge on another man's space. But it was a good-sized square; Rowan could barely hear the other instrument from where he stood. Likely, neither of them would make as much as they would without the competition, but Rowan could live with that.

He climbed into the caravan and emerged with a small stool and a large case. He settled himself down, drew out the button box and wrapped the whole contraption inside his jacket, trying to get enough warmth into the pleated leather bellows to ensure they wouldn't crack when he stretched them out.

"Get out of here!" The voice was an angry hiss right next to his head. Startled, Rowan looked up to find the fiddler looming over him. Two high spots of color burned in his narrow face. The pale blue eyes were cold and angry.

"I..." Rowan cleared his throat. His voice had long since dropped, but it still had a tendency to betray him in heated moments. "I beg your pardon?"

The older boy straightened and waved a peremptory arm. "Clear out. I was here first. You'll drown me out with that thing."

That thing? Now Rowan was angry. "There's plenty of room for both of us, and what you are calling *that thing* is a premium brass-tongued button box, made by the master, Reed Blackbird himself!" His button box was the most valuable thing his family owned, and other musicians, at least, should recognize its quality.

This one was unimpressed. "Yes, yes, I heard one before. Sounds like a dying seagull." He pointed a threatening finger. "Pack up your little squawk box and move on." He turned and stalked, storklike, back to his spot with his fiddle tucked under one arm.

Rowan watched, seething with anger and indecision, while the young man set out his open case and began to play. He wasn't afraid of a fight, not really. Though taller, the fiddler was slightly built and didn't look that strong. But the dog gave Rowan pause, and now the moment for defending his claim seemed to have passed. Reluctantly, he laid the button box back in its case.

Heska's teeth, he thought with disgust, the guy wasn't even any good. He was dogging through a basic reel now in a way that set Rowan's teeth on edge. There was something weird about his playing, something he couldn't quite put his finger on...

Rowan made a sudden decision, stowed his box in the caravan and began to sidle through the edges of the crowd until he was close enough to get a good look at—and earful of—his rival.

The more he watched, the more curious he became. Lately, Rowan hadn't cared much about anything except eating and staying warm, but this boy...he was a mystery.

He was dressed well, or had been once. The style was odd, brighter and more dramatically cut than Rowan was used to, but well tailored. His coat, Rowan thought enviously, looked really warm. But it was dirty too, and the boy's pants were muddied at the hems.

His playing was full of contradictions as well. He wasn't a hack, as Rowan had first assumed. You could tell by the light, loose way he held the bow, its smooth draw across the strings and the sweet tone he got from his instrument. He'd had training, all right. Yet something was seriously wrong. He had moved on to a jig, another standard that any pub player could manage. What was wrong with it? The notes were all there, but the tune had no movement, no rhythm, nothing to make you want to tap your toe or nod your head.

Well, he wouldn't be making much money with that, especially with his haughty manner. He didn't even acknowledge the few coppers that people tossed in his fiddle case but just stared into space as he played. Rowan had no qualms about setting up in his own corner with some real music.

He was halfway across the square when a new sound stopped him. It pricked up the hair on the back on his neck and brought the gooseflesh out on his arms.

Eyes wide, every ounce of his attention claimed, he turned back to the blond stranger.

He had never heard such music. Jigs and reels and shuffles—toe-tapping, foot-stomping dance music—those he knew. And the slow airs—beautiful, keening melodies for love won and lost, laments and longings—he knew those as well. But he had never heard a fiddle sob and wail like this.

The fiddle swooped up and held a long, tremulous note. And then, with a rhythmic sway like a woman's hips rolling, it prowled down the minor scale and landed with a wild discord that was heartbreak and rage all at once. It was as though the mute pain that lay trapped in Rowan's chest had at last been given a voice, and for a moment he was horrified to find himself giving way to tears.

He pulled himself back into the music—gods above, it was mesmerizing. The tall blond musician was transformed in Rowan's eyes, the hostility and bad manners forgotten. Rowan listened, motionless, through two long compositions, until his ear began to understand the unfamiliar sound.

The crowd, he noticed, did not share his reaction. Their faces were startled or bemused, not transported. No one was rushing to fill the fiddle case. An idea—an idea that quickly grew as compelling as the music—came to him.

Rowan hurried to the caravan and pulled out the skin drum. No time to check the tension—it would have to do. Grabbing the stool, he scurried back around the edge of the square, approaching the stranger from behind. Intent on his strange music, he didn't notice Rowan until the smiles and pointing fingers of the passersby drew his attention.

Rowan expected—and got—an indignant glare, but he just nodded and smiled and motioned to the other boy to continue. "Perhaps we can make a little more coin together," he suggested. "You aren't doing so well on your own."

It was like watching the ruff on a rooster rise and then smooth as the truth of Rowan's words hit home. With a quick, surly nod, the fiddler returned to his playing. A few bars later, once he was sure of the rhythm, Rowan joined in.

FOUR

Rowan had wondered what he would do if his new partner refused to share their earnings, but the blond stranger divided up the coins scrupulously, waving away Rowan's suggestion that he first take out those he had earned alone.

"You were right. I did better this way." He passed Rowan a handful of coins and curtly offered his name along with them. "I am Aydin."

"Rowan."

Aydin acknowledged the introduction with a nod and a smile that verged on a sneer.

"Something funny about my name?" Aydin's manners grated on Rowan as badly as his jigs.

But the tall boy was shaking his head, waving his hand back and forth to smooth over Rowan's annoyance.

"No, no. I just find it odd—how you people name things after other things."

"What's so odd about that?" Rowan had been named for a tree said in olden times to dance when a master musician played. It was a favored name in musical families, and Rowan had always been proud to bear it.

"It's not a proper name, is it? It's something else's name! Even your country—Prosper. It's not a name, it's just some childish wish that if you call a place a certain thing, then it will be so."

Irritated and strangely tongue-tied—how do you even argue whether a name is a name?—Rowan was about to retreat into surly silence when something Aydin had said wakened his curiosity, dormant these long lonely months.

"Wait a minute. You said Prosper was *my* country. So where are *you* from?"

Rowan had not noticed any particular accent in Aydin's speech, but other observations were falling into place—his clothing, the golden tone to his skin that made him look like he'd just spent a summer outdoors. He was not especially surprised, then, at the reply.

"I am Tarzine." The tall boy grinned, looked conspiratorially up and down the square, and bent close to Rowan, his white-blond hair falling forward and screening his face. "Don't tell anyone."

CURIOSITY AND LONELINESS made Rowan reluctant to part company, even with someone as abrasive as Aydin. And so he found himself suggesting that they pool their money and buy some food at the market for a shared dinner in the caravan.

"So you live here?" asked Aydin as Rowan struggled with the rusty padlock at the door. The tone of cool disdain made Rowan regret his invitation.

"I do now." Rowan suppressed the urge to boast about how spacious and comfortable his family's lodgings at Five Oaks, the estate of the Earl of East Brockwood, had been. In truth, that seemed a lifetime ago, or maybe only a wistful dream. He pushed open the door and turned to the older boy. "You don't have to come in if it's beneath you."

Aydin paid no mind to Rowan's sharp reply. He stepped in, glanced up and down the length of the caravan and nodded slowly. "It's better lodgings than I've had lately," he said and flashed Rowan another of those disarming grins. "Last night I gave the scullery maid at the inn a copper to sneak me into the root cellar."

Rowan didn't know what to make of the man. He sneered at everything, and then just when you were ready to plug him upside the head, you'd get that grin, as if it was all just a friendly joke. Not knowing what to say, he said nothing and instead busied himself with the stove and pots.

Aydin had not been impressed with Rowan's frugal market purchases of lentils, barley and onions, insisting on adding a hefty chunk of bacon, but he did not stint in the eating of it. Between Aydin and his huge dog, a stew that would have fed Rowan's entire family and a couple of guests besides was soon reduced to an empty dog-licked pot. Blessedly, all that intense eating meant that Rowan was spared the inevitable questions until after.

"We'll have life stories over tea," Aydin announced, rummaging in his pack and producing a crumpled, much-folded parchment envelope. "There's a little left here."

"So let's start with the caravan." Aydin's eyes again swept the length of the covered wagon, resting for a moment on the black stain on the floorboards. The sun was going down, but it was comfortable enough at the tiny table beside the stove, which Rowan had resolved to leave in its metal housing in the galley from now on. The evening was calm, and the dog, splayed out on the floor, didn't mind serving as a footwarmer.

"It's not much of a house. Still, it's not often you see a boy of—what, twelve years?"

"Sixteen," growled Rowan, adding one to his true count.

"—in sole possession of a caravan, not to mention the mules and several valuable instruments. So I'm guessing this is your family's—yes?"

Rowan forced his mouth around the next words. "It was my family's. They died early in the winter."

"Ah." Aydin nodded, as though he had expected as much. He didn't fall over himself to gush out his sympathy, and for that Rowan was grateful. "An accident?"

Of course the nosy bugger wouldn't leave it alone. Rowan sighed. Aydin did not backtrack (*I'm sorry, I didn't mean to pry…*) but merely waited.

"They died of the plague. It cropped up in the castle where my parents were the resident musicians, and we didn't get out in time."

Now he had Aydin's full attention, the ice-blue eyes round and probing.

"And you didn't get it?"

"I did get it." Rowan's voice was flat, striving—and failing—to say the words without conjuring the memory. "I just didn't die."

HE HAD BEEN TRYING TO BURY his father, Cashel, when he realized that he was sick himself. It was impossible work—Cashel had taken them far away from Five Oaks and down a rutted, overgrown trail leading deep into the woods so that they wouldn't spread the disease if they were overcome. Now, with nothing but an ax and a manure shovel, Rowan was trying to hack his way into the stubborn webbing of half-frozen root and rock that protected the soil.

It took no time at all to realize he would fail, and this somehow seemed a worse blow than the horror that had come before: his father, so terribly *absent*, the gray, ravaged face hardly recognizable in its utter blankness; his mother and sister tossing and moaning in their bunks, witless with fever. Ettie's cries cut like a shrill knife in his ears. The stench of disease bloated the air of the cramped caravan. There was nothing he could do about any of it, except this one thing: to see the dead decently buried. And even that it seemed, was too much to ask. He would have to leave his father out here in the open, prey to the elements and scavengers.

With a howl of rage, grief and fear, Rowan fell on the earth with his ax, raining down a flurry of blows that hacked a shallow V into the earth before the blade hit a rock and nearly bucked out of his hands. He was sweating and shivering with exertion and emotion, his face running with snot and tears. He bent from the waist, sucking air that seemed suddenly too thin. A bolt of pain stabbed in his head, a wave of black dizziness in its wake. And as he slowly lowered the ax to the ground, he felt it—a pain in his armpit where the skin rubbed together, a tender, sore swelling that he realized had been bothering him even when he was wrapping his father in his blankets and dragging him out the door. Rowan tottered over to the caravan and lowered himself onto the step. His head pounded, as though the ax had attacked his skull rather than the earth. Reluctantly, knowing already what he would find, he worked his hand under his tunic and up to the sleeve.

The lump was a hot, hard, poisoned egg under his skin. His heart lurched with fear as his fingers probed. Slowly, he lifted the hem of his tunic and gazed down at his exposed skin. There they were, the hateful "plague kisses": blotchy purple circles blooming over his belly.

So that was it. They would all die—his mother and Ettie, and finally Rowan himself, gasping out his last breath in the company of corpses. Their hurried flight had been pointless. Rowan wondered, without really caring, how many lay ill at the castle and whether it was spreading beyond its walls. It was the earl's eldest son, Lapis, recently returned from a trading voyage, who had brought the disease in. They had all played at his homecoming feast, but Rowan's father had been asked to attend the young lord again the next evening, to help him set to music some scraps of poetry he had written at sea. The night had been cut short—to Cashel's relief— when Lapis said a headache was making it impossible to concentrate. By dawn the young man lay in the grip of fever, the buboes swelling in his armpit and groin, and Rowan's father had somehow got the news and was packing madly before the rest of them awoke. But it was already too late.

Rowan rested his head in his hands and tried to think. There were things he should do while he still could. Untether the mules, so they would have a hope of surviving until some passerby found himself a free team. Fill the water bucket. It was weird how calm he felt, now that they were all in the same boat. The barely suppressed panic that had twisted his guts for days was gone. It seemed easier to die himself than to watch helplessly while the others suffered.

By the time he climbed back into the caravan with the fresh water, his legs trembled at the effort, and the press of his arm, weighted with the full bucket, was a torment against his swelling armpit. He poured water into the drinking pitcher and urged a few swallows into Ettie. The heat poured off her, and she mewled in pain as he lifted up her sweaty head. The glands in her neck—like stones bulging from her skin—had discolored to a dark, angry purple. But she drank thirstily. Then he dipped a towel into the bucket, wrung it out and dabbed it over her face.

Rowan did the same for his mother, Hazel, and that was all he could manage. Unhooking his bunk, he pulled it down on its hinge and climbed in. The pain in his head washed over him in waves, an onrushing tide. "Just let me sleep," he muttered. "Dear Somos, kindest god, just let me sleep a little before the worst of it."

Rowan tried to tell himself that he didn't remember much after that—but he remembered enough. He remembered the harsh, bloody cough that began tearing itself from his mother's chest and the terrifying red spray that she tried, at first, to contain in her blanket. He saw then how her fingers were turning black with the inner bleeding. Later she was too weak even to wipe the foamy bright dribble from her cheeks, her eyes and temples mottled with bruises. Soon after that, the fever took him so fiercely, he was aware of nothing but his own throbbing head and quaking chills.

And he remembered the searing pain when the swollen bubo under his arm burst. His own scream woke him, and he had thought he must be dying, not noticing at first that the pain was already seeping away with the putrid fluid staining his nightshirt. The stench was awful, but to Rowan's relief, he was able to shrug out of the shirt and wad it up for a bandage. He sat like that, dazed from his long, dark dreams, and it gradually came to him that he felt better.

Trembly with weakness, dizzy, headachy—but better. Stretching out his arm, he managed to grasp his water mug and take a careful sip. Gods, it was good. Greedily he sucked down the rest, then fell back into his bed and into a true sleep.

He put off getting out of bed for as long as he could, unable to face what he knew waited for him. The silence had already smothered any hope.

Ettie lay pale but composed, as though she had laid herself out before dying. *She looks so small*, thought Rowan—even smaller than in life. *My sister*. He touched a blond braid, then her cheek. But it wasn't her— not anymore. Ettie's cheeks had been warm, dimpled, never still like this under your hand. And then he was sobbing, his head pressed into the edge of her bunk, the enormity of loss crushing his heart.

But his mother's body waited. She had not gone quietly to the deadlands. Bloodstained and livid with bruises, she looked as though her final battle had been against bludgeon and knife.

There was no part of her he could bear to touch. Mumbling out a prayer for her safe passage, Rowan untucked her bedsheets and wrapped first one side, then the other over his mother's body.

By the time he had dragged first his mother's, then his sister's, wrapped bodies out of the caravan and laid them beside his father on the frozen ground, Rowan was near to collapse. Slow and shaky as an old man, he made his way back to his bunk. His ragged, helpless weeping seemed like it would never stop, until at last his exhausted body took over and merciful sleep carried him away.

THE SILENCE STRETCHED OUT as Rowan stared into the red innards of the stove, trapped in his memories.

Aydin's next question pulled him back.

"So I guess that girl is your sister then?"

Rowan tried to make sense of the question. He looked around the walls of the caravan, looking for a picture he knew did not exist. Aydin sipped his tea and waited calmly, his pale eyes unblinking.

Finally Rowan gave up. "What are you talking about? What girl?"

"The girl who hovers about you." Aydin shrugged, unconcerned. "Perhaps you do not see her." He gave one of his superior smiles. "It would not surprise me."

Rowan's reaction was so violent and confused, he couldn't speak: Rage at Aydin's callousness, to toy with him so. Grief like a black ocean for the little girl who had tagged at his heels. And beneath it all whispered a superstitious, hair-prickling dread, as his traitor mind babbled, *But what if...*

"What's wrong with you?" The words burst out of him like a curse. "Why would you say a thing like that? Can you not even respect the dead?"

Aydin took a sip of tea as though nothing had been said. The smile—a smile Rowan was very close to wiping from his face, dog or no dog—did not falter. And when

Rowan sputtered into silence, Aydin put his tea down, sat back in his chair and looked him straight in the eye.

"She's small, about up to your chest. She has fair hair—not as light as mine, but blond—in two long plaits. She has a round face, round cheeks."

That means nothing, thought Rowan, though shivery chills were crawling up and down his spine. *Lots of girls have braids. He's bluffing.*

"She wears a purple gemstone at her neck."

Ettie. Sweet gods of earth and air, it was Ettie. Rowan had won that lump of amethyst for her at a fair, and she had loved it so much that their father had paid to have a silver-smith fix it to a small loop so she could string it around her neck. She had worn that stone for the last three years. She had died wearing it.

FIVE

Rowan's mind seethed with questions he didn't seem to be able to ask, foremost among them, *Is she here now?* He gazed down the dark length of the caravan, fighting the shivers crawling up his spine, trying to compose himself enough to say something that didn't sound absurd. He couldn't.

"You seem astonished," Aydin remarked.

"Of course I'm astonished! What else would I be?" Rowan heard the husky crack in his voice and for once didn't care.

Aydin shrugged, a languid ripple quite unlike the gesture Rowan thought of as "a shrug."

"You've never heard of a ghost? Your language has the word—there must be a concept to match."

Of course he had heard of ghosts. But ghosts weren't *here*—they were denizens of the deadlands. Only in rare dreams did Somos open a connection to allow the dead and the living to make contact.

But how did he know that? Rowan hadn't had an especially religious upbringing. His parents had maintained a shrine to Heska, god of music, in their home at Five Oaks—a shrine, he thought with a stab of uneasy guilt, he should set up himself in the caravan—and on their summer travels they would make a small offering to the local deity when occasion demanded. But as far as the theology of death and the afterlife went, Rowan's "knowledge" was based largely on the ritual words uttered at the handful of funeral rites he had played at.

Was she here now?

It was more than he could deal with. He had heard her, he realized, that night in the caravan. *Rowan,* she had called. *Rowan.* It wasn't a dream—he had heard her. She had saved him from the fire. Ettie.

Abruptly, Rowan pushed back the stool and stood up. "It's late. I'm going to bed."

Aydin raised an eyebrow but said nothing. He unfolded himself slowly from his seat and made for the door. "Then I'll thank you for dinner and be on my way."

A cool breath on his neck made Rowan turn up his collar. It was colder even a few steps away from the stove. Much colder outside, no doubt.

Another gust, short and sharp, like a push. No draft he had ever felt had given him such a feeling. Nerves, no doubt—that spooky Tarzine had given him the willies.

Still, he found himself clearing his throat and asking brusquely, "You have a place to stay?"

"I will find one. It's not your concern."

Great. For the first time since his family's death, Rowan really wanted to be alone. But he could imagine all too well how it would feel to be turned out of a caravan, however chilly, into a winter's night.

"Look, you can stay here if you want. It won't be that comfortable, but there's lots of room."

Aydin gazed at him appraisingly, as if to divine whether the offer was genuine. He accepted with another shrug.

"I suppose if I was going to catch the plague from staying here, I've already got it."

"You don't have to worry about that." The prefect of the first town Rowan had come to after his recovery had seen to that. Rowan had thought at the time it was his youth, and the fact that he was alone, that had brought a town official asking after his business. Now he realized it was his haggard appearance, the burden of illness still plain on his face, that attracted attention. Nobody had questioned his entry into a town for weeks now.

That first prefect had recoiled three full steps when Rowan spoke the word *plague*, innocently assuming that if the bodies had been left behind, so had the danger. From behind a face covered first by a spread, pudgy hand and then with a hastily produced handkerchief, the prefect said curtly, "Go outside the city walls immediately—well outside! Stay in your caravan and wait for me there."

It had been a long, anxious wait before a small squad of people (none of them the prefect) arrived, faces swaddled in shawls, with oil, bundles of kindling and two barrels of vinegar. Rowan had been told to burn mattresses, blankets, clothing—anything an ill person, including himself, might have touched. Only the four extra blankets in their box were spared, and these only when Rowan swore under oath they had not been touched since the previous winter. The entire inside of the caravan was then soaked and scrubbed in vinegar. He slept in the fumes and awoke feeling like he'd been pickled. Only the next day was he allowed in town to buy breakfast and busk for coins.

In the next town, despite clear evidence that he had already cleaned everything, he was made to scrub down the caravan again. After that, he told anyone who asked that his father had been robbed and killed coming home one night in the port town of Shiphaven, and that if he himself looked sickly, it was only from shock and grief and having too little to eat. It was a good story that sometimes earned him donated food as well as a sympathetic audience. Still, it was a relief when people stopped asking and he could enter a town without bracing himself for the questions.

"You won't have a mattress, I'm afraid," he told Aydin now. "They've all been burned. And I managed to burn a couple more blankets awhile back." The blankets smelled unpleasantly of charred wool but were still in one piece. "We can fold the burnt ones into pads to sleep on and have a good blanket each on top."

He piled blankets into Aydin's arms as he talked, the busy work of hosting a welcome distraction. The tall boy cast an uncertain look around the caravan.

"That one." Rowan pointed to the broad platform at the far end of the caravan—his parents' bed. Ettie's was too close and besides...Rowan gave himself a mental shake, but the thought persisted. If she *was* here—and he couldn't imagine how or why she could be, but if she was—well, he wasn't about to let anybody else sleep in her bed. If that was crazy, so be it.

"It's really cold down here."

Rowan briefly reconsidered giving Aydin Ettie's bunk, or moving the stove onto the floor closer to the beds but rejected both ideas.

"Good thing you have a big dog," he said.

And, as if he understood, the great beast heaved himself from the floor, padded down the caravan and flopped sideways across the blanket Aydin had just laid down for a mattress.

"His name is K'waaf." A snort of derisive amusement. "But in keeping with local tradition in the prosperous land of Prosper, I call him Wolf."

ROWAN SLEPT POORLY and rose early, tired of lying in his hard bunk thinking—or trying not to think—about Ettie. He would buy a mattress with the money he had found, emergency or not, he thought. He was too young to feel so stiff each morning.

He stuck his nose experimentally into the gray dawn. It was damp and misty, with a bank of cloud lowering over the town. A rainy day to come, he guessed, and poor prospects for playing or traveling. The market square was deserted in the half-light, the streets silent but for the occasional banging of a shutter or door and a burst of raucous shrieking of crows from—Rowan craned his neck, following the sound—maybe the bell tower? Sure enough, a flapping black form rose from the structure in a swell of sound, as though ejected by the sheer force of its neighbors' cawing. It settled on the pinnacle, only to be jostled off by a second crow. "Doing their best to scare the sun back under the world," his father used to complain.

That was about ravens, not crows, he reminded himself, and then the memory was back, live and present and crushing in its loneliness. It was a family story, one they used to laugh about together, and Rowan could not imagine how he would ever laugh about it again. He had been nine or ten. Still using the old button box, and just starting to join his parents for selected tunes or easy engagements. They had traveled in the caravan to the calving festival in Grassy Creek, and arrived late to find a very crowded camp area surrounding the festival grounds. His mother had been worried. "We might have to stay off the grounds," she said. She liked the caravan easily accessible for meals, and his father liked it close by so he could keep an eye out for thieves. Then his father had pointed triumphantly to a lovely big site under an ancient beech tree. There was room for four caravans there at least, and they hurried to claim the shady area closest to the trunk.

It wasn't until the next morning, when the ravens let loose a dawn chorus from the top branches of the tree loud enough to wake the dead, that the family understood why no one had joined them in their prime camping spot. "Like birds, do you?" an old man—a rope seller, Rowan found out later—had asked them with a wink and a broad grin as they were setting up. Each morning, as the late nights piled up, the ravens became harder to endure until finally the dawn broke when Rowan's father leaped out of bed and started yelling back at them in a crude but passable imitation of their exuberant, ear-splitting calls. Soon Rowan and Ettie were shrieking and giggling, flapping from one bunk to another in awkward leaps.

Rowan smiled, remembering. When he realized he was smiling, he felt guilty. He would never be able to tease his father about those birds again—and with that realization, the grief came again and broke over him like a wave.

"Why don't you just shut up," he muttered, glaring at the bell tower.

He needed breakfast. Good thing he'd held back that loaf of bread from Aydin and his giant dog.

six

Samik sniffed at the steaming cup Rowan handed him—
not a true tea, just hot water with a few dried bergamot
leaves thrown in—and pointedly set it aside. Surely Rowan
didn't consider this drinkable?

"So," he said, leaning back and folding his arms. "Your
turn now to ask the questions."

Rowan fidgeted in his chair. The little twitch in his right
eye, the one Samik had first noticed when Rowan was telling
the appalling story of his family's death, had started up again.
Rowan was dying to ask more about his sister's ghost, that was
obvious. Yet he had also been violently upset at Samik's obser-
vation and had abruptly changed the subject. Samik wondered
if he'd stumbled into some primitive Backender taboo.

"If you're Tarzine, why don't you have an accent?" Rowan
finally blurted out.

"That's easy. My mother is a Backender. She taught me."

"A what?"

"A Backender." Samik shrugged. "It is what we call you. Because you have the back end of the Island."

Extraordinary. Samik watched Rowan's face redden as he seemed to go through some internal struggle—could he really be about to start an argument about which end was the *back* end? But whatever was angering him, he dropped it and instead asked, "Then how did your parents meet?"

"My father saw her in the slave market in Baskir, and was so struck by her beauty—especially her pale blond hair, a rare color in our lands—that he bought her. Soon after, he set her free, and soon after that they were married."

Rowan suddenly looked as if he had bitten down on something vile, and Samik felt his stomach tighten. He had seen this reaction before, had learned in fact to tell only his most deeply trusted friends about his mother's past. But there was no slavery in Prosper, and he hadn't thought to find such prejudice here.

"Your mother was a *slave?*"

"I have told you she was." It was Samik's turn to be angry now, his voice cold and tight.

"A Prosperian citizen, sold as a slave?"

He had misunderstood. It wasn't disdain for his slave mother he was seeing, it was some kind of national outrage. How simpleminded to think slavery was somehow *worse* for Prosperians!

"Why not?" he answered. "Slavers don't care who you are. Our own people are taken."

"So you don't agree with the slave trade?"

"Of course I do not." Samik glared at him, the pale eyes so fierce that Rowan hesitated before he spoke again.

"But your father…"

"My father does not keep slaves. He bought a person he could not stand to see in chains and freed her. She is not the only one he has freed. He knows this does nothing to fight the trade itself, but he is an emotional person and sometimes his heart wins over his head." Samik offered a frosty smile. "My mother, at least, is glad that it does."

"Fine. Sorry." Rowan made a show of slicing more bread and refilling his cup, and Samik relished his little victory.

"Next question?" Rowan looked rather startled at Samik's willingness to continue, and he hesitated before diving in once more.

"Well, then. What are you doing here in Prosper?"

"Ah." *At last, something worth talking about.* "That is a very long story, and I will need more than this dishwashing swill to get me through it. Do you have any spirits?"

"Spirits?" Rowan's eyes grew round, and Samik remembered with amusement that the word *spirits* had two meanings.

"Wine, ale, brandy. Corn mash in a pinch—maybe I could put some in with these gray leaves…"

"Oh, that. I'm afraid it's all gone. I—well, I finished it one night when I couldn't sleep."

"Did it work?"

A wan smile. "Made me sick, mostly."

Oh, this boy was such an easy target, it was almost impossible to resist teasing him. But there was a story to be told, and unlike Rowan, who had shared his history with painful reluctance, Samik was eager to tell it. He had come to realize that confiding in Missus Broadbeam was a mistake. She knew things about him that might help Jago's men, in the unlikely event that they traced him to her. But it wasn't natural to keep everything to yourself, day after day. Luckily, Rowan was on the move himself. They would never find him to question.

"On the day I left home," Samik began, "I was wakened at an ungodly hour when my little brother landed on my head." He put on a shrill, high-pitched voice in imitation: "'Samik, wake up! Samik, wake up! Samik, wake—'" Samik paused, noticing Rowan's confusion. "Samik is me," he explained. "Aydin is my maternal grandfather's name. I borrowed it for this…journey."

Rowan nodded, and Samik continued. "I was about to smother him with my pillow when he said, 'Father wants you in the cellar as soon as you're ready,' and I remembered what day it was.

"My father, Ziv, is a wine merchant. Not the biggest, but the most exclusive. We supply wines to Emperor Nazir himself." It was a great honor to supply the emperor, and Samik was proud of his father's achievement. But Rowan's sour look suggested he was not just unimpressed but even annoyed.

Samik couldn't imagine why Rowan would begrudge his family this success. He wondered if all Backenders were this prickly, or if Rowan's countrymen found him difficult too. With a mental shake, he brought himself back to his story.

"Not all of my father's customers are, let's say, *loyal supporters* of the empire." And some, he thought to himself, are nearly as powerful and far more dangerous than the emperor himself…

THE WARLORD JAGO, who ruled over the inner badlands south of the River Hanajim, was arriving this day to place his annual order. The household was in an uproar—Jago was an important and difficult customer, a lavish spender notorious for his vicious temper. Samik had been up late with his father the night before, ensuring the cellar was in perfect order while Ziv reviewed his selection and order of offerings and double-checked that each bottle and glass was spotless. Samik's mother and his Aunt Kir, who lived with them, had driven their staff into a frenzy of housecleaning and cooking and shopping, for while the warlord rarely left Ziv's office on his visits, there must be a range of delicacies available to sample with the wines, and there was always the possibility he would decide to stay on for a meal, which would then have to be produced instantly. It was no exaggeration to say an underdone piece of trout could ruin the whole deal with this man.

Before Jago's arrival, Samik's eight-year-old brother, Merik, was shooed off in the care of a young maid named Elida so he wouldn't be underfoot. "Two birds with one stone," said his mother triumphantly as she sent them out the door.

"What's that, my dear?" Ziv was only half listening, preoccupied with the business to come.

"You probably didn't notice the way Jago stared at Elida last year—but I did. The poor girl felt like a suckling pig about to be eaten," said Samik's mother. "Just as well she'll be out of sight today."

The meeting went off without a hitch. Samik served while the two men talked, sniffed and tasted. He knew the routine in his sleep, but most customers were unlikely to care about a sloppy pour or a misplaced napkin. He was nervous, feeling it in the tightness of his stomach and the tremor in his fingers. But he managed not to fumble or spill anything, and his father's strategy—to hold back the best for last and introduce it as "something special I have been saving for you, Lord Jago"—worked perfectly, adding a lucrative incremental sale on top of an already large order.

"As soon as possible, mind," Jago cautioned, as they followed him up the cellar stairs. He was a big man, not tall but wide, and his broad shoulders and barrel chest nearly filled the narrow stairwell. Samik had a sudden vision of the man missing a step and crushing them both like a boulder as he fell, and he had to suppress the urge to fall back a few paces.

"If you will allow Samik to escort you to your carriage, I will make arrangements immediately, my lord." Though making it seem like a service, his father would be all too happy to comply—*sooner shipped, sooner paid* was one of his favorite mottoes.

"Do so." Jago paused on the stairs, breathing heavily. "Damn this business, with its underground storage. They should invent a wine that thrives in the light of day."

"Indeed, my lord." Ziv was too smart to point out that most customers were content to sit in the ground-floor office and have sample bottles brought up to them; it was Jago himself who insisted on visiting the cellars and choosing the specific bottle from each vintage to sample, saying, "So I know what I'm drinking is what I am buying."

Samik trailed after the warlord as he proceeded to the front door—the man knew the way perfectly well and hardly needed an escort. His mother waited to greet Jago, curtseying prettily and enduring it graciously when he grabbed her by the waist, puckered up and smacked her noisily on both cheeks. *As close to the mouth as he could manage*, Samik thought with disgust, but he held his peace.

Jago's carriage awaited in the cobbled street beyond the gate. "Allow me, my lord," said Samik, as he darted ahead to hold the gate open. Jago went through and headed for the carriage door his man held waiting. "A pleasure doing business with you, my lord," Samik said to the back of Jago's head. But the man had already forgotten him.

Jago had one foot on the step of his carriage when Merik came flying down the street, howling like a dervish from the Forbidden Caves. Head down, hands clapped over one eye, he showed no sign of seeing the three people standing in his way.

"Merik, watch out!" Samik shouted, but it was too late. His brother ran smack into Jago's broad backside. The man looked immovable as a mountain, but he must have been off his balance, because he fell right on top of the bawling boy.

Elida came puffing up in Merik's wake. "He got a hornet sting," she began and then stopped in confused shock and growing horror.

Samik and the coachman, who had both jumped in to help, were thrown back violently by a snarling Jago. The coachman resumed his station by the coach steps, face stony, eyes averted. Samik stood back warily, waiting for the big man to rise so he could scoop Merik into the house.

But he didn't rise. With a string of curses, he turned on the boy pinned underneath him and began to beat him.

It was pandemonium—Jago bellowing, Merik crying and struggling, Samik and the maid both shouting at the warlord to stop. Samik's mother came flying out the door, jumped in and began hauling on the big man's shoulders, trying to pry him off her boy. Samik leaped in to help, but Jago was heavy and strong, his rage growing rather than spending itself, and they could not shift him. He had his hands around Merik's neck now, shaking the boy up and down like a rag doll. Samik's mother began shrieking at him and raining blows on his head, but she might as well have been a mosquito for all the notice he took. Merik was not crying anymore—he was blue and silent, eyes bulging in terror. Jago was killing him.

Samik cast around desperately for some kind of weapon. He could pry up a cobblestone—no, it would take too long. Merik's life was surely now measured in seconds, not minutes. There was all kinds of debris on the street, but none of it heavy enough to—

The house idol. He sat in his tiny alcove cut into the wall beside the front door, eight thumbs of solid stone, supposedly protecting the home from thieves. Well, he could protect them now.

Samik snatched the stone idol from its base and raced back to Jago. Merik was unconscious now. *God of all gods, let him be unconscious, not dead,* thought Samik. He raised the idol and brought it down with all his strength on the back of the warlord's head. The crunch, Jago's collapse onto the cobblestones, the blood staining around his head, all seemed to happen in a slow, silent dream.

And then things happened very fast indeed. He vaguely heard his mother calling servants, sending for the bonesetter, ordering his brother and Jago to be carried inside. But Samik was inside before anyone else, yanked in the door and dragged into the cellar by his father, who muttered at him, "Lie low here until I come back for you." He was in trouble, he knew that. If Jago died, he had committed murder, and though it would surely be found to be justified, Jago's clansmen were not likely to leave his punishment to a judge. And if he lived…

If Jago lives, I'm a dead man. Samik was scared now, really scared. The man was a warlord—for the first time,

Samik really considered what that meant, and the inherent risk of doing business with such a man. A warlord with a murderous temper. There was no way for an ordinary person to protect himself against a warlord with a grudge— and Jago would hold a grudge all right. He would hold it for as long as it took to get satisfaction.

Samik's father had evidently come to the same conclusion, for he hurried down the stairs a short time later carrying a travel bag and Samik's cloak.

"They're both alive," he replied to Samik's first question. "The bonesetter says Merik will live, but he can't say if..." His voice faltered, and he gulped in a couple of fast breaths. His father was close to crying, Samik realized, and that scared him more than everything else.

"He can't say," his father repeated, deliberately now, "if he will be all right, or if he might be damaged in the head."

Damaged in the head. The words were ominous, but Samik didn't quite know what they meant. While he debated the wisdom of asking, his father stepped up to him and clutched him in a hard hug. "He is only alive because of you," Ziv whispered. "You have our eternal thanks, your mother's and mine. But you have put yourself in great danger."

"Jago—how is he?" Samik asked. His father shook his head.

"Still unconscious. He looks likely to live but...same as Merik. You broke his skull with that statue. He might recover and be his same old evil self, or he might end up unable to speak, or weak in his legs…or crazy." His father gave a strained bark of laughter. "Though as we just saw, he is already crazy."

"He'll come after me if he can, won't he?"

Ziv nodded. "As sure as morning follows night. Samik, you'll have to leave. The man can hire the best assassins in the country—and he will. The only way I can think to keep you alive is to make you disappear."

"Where will I go?"

Ziv was counting out coins as he spoke. "Go to your mother's land—Jago's spy network will not extend so far. I've sent for a hire coach, so it won't be identified as mine. It will take you to Guara harbor. From there you can get on a trade ship to—well, anywhere in Prosper will do. They mostly go to Shiphaven. Take the first one you can get."

Samik nodded mechanically, trying to make his mind think ahead when it wanted to be stunned and stupid. He slung the purse his father gave him around his neck and tucked it inside his tunic, then stood holding a second pouch, unsure of where to stash it.

"Take K'waaf," his father said. "He'll protect you with his life."

"How long will I stay?"

"I don't know, Samik." His father looked worried. "It will be longer than your money will last. You'll need to find a way to earn more."

"I'll take my viol," said Samik. At least it would be a good place to hide the extra money. "Didn't Mother always say the Backenders love music and pay a good penny to hear it?"

Ziv nodded. "It's a start. There isn't time for a better plan—the magistrate's men will be here before long, and you must be gone when they arrive."

When Ziv returned with the viol case and a leather dog lead, Samik shrugged into his coat and slung the bag over his shoulder. "What did you pack in there, anyway?"

"Not much," his father confessed. "Clothes, a map of Prosper that your mother keeps and—well, I tossed in a couple of small bottles." He smiled weakly. "Thought they might be fortifying."

Samik hitched a deep breath, trying to grasp the fact that he was about to walk out the door, leave his family and head into an unknown land. "Is the coach here?"

His father nodded. "In the back alley. Go out the scullery door and take the dog from the kennel on your way. Hopefully Jago and his men don't know about K'waaf."

They stood awkwardly. "How will I know when...?" Samik began. His father lifted his hands helplessly.

"If Jago recovers, this house will be watched. I don't know...give it three moon cycles anyway. Then, if you have landed in a place where you can stay for a while, try to send a message. If it's safe for you to return, I'll send word— or come and get you myself."

That was the last Samik had seen of his family.

SEVEN

Rowan had been so absorbed in Aydin's story that it took him a minute to realize that it was done. Incredible, that such violence and menace could just break into a family's life. Imagine living in a country where "warlords" were an everyday reality…

Aydin stretched out his long legs and propped them, crossed at the ankle, on the empty chair and yawned hugely. *Ettie's chair*, thought Rowan, but Ettie wouldn't have minded. Besides, he wasn't done with Aydin's story.

"How long have you—?"

"About a fortnight," said Aydin cheerfully. "And already I am nearly out of money. My education in frugal living has been woefully inadequate, I'm afraid." He sat up straighter and looked hopefully around the little scullery. "Kiar's Great Ax, I'm hungry. Is there any…?"

"Not a scrap," Rowan said firmly. "Not for you or for Kiar, whoever that is." He hadn't been bothering with a midday meal lately, through indifference as much as thrift, but now his stomach growled its agreement with Aydin. Damn the man; he'd felt fine before Aydin mentioned food.

"Look, I have an idea," Rowan ventured. "We're stuck here for today anyway, so why don't we try to find some music we can play together and try our luck at the inn tonight?"

"There are two," Aydin offered. "If the first won't feed us, we'll try the other."

Two inns. Rowan groaned inwardly; he could have done perfectly well on his own in one inn and left the other to Aydin, with no need to feel guilty. Now he was stuck with a partner who played exquisite music completely unsuited to the little rural towns that dotted this part of the country. "Fine," he said. "My point is we should practice together."

"Yes, yes." Aydin flapped a hand up and down dismissively, and Rowan felt his face tighten with anger.

"I can't play on an empty stomach. Wait here and I'll see what I can scramble up." Aydin was shrugging into his heavy coat as he spoke. He turned the collar up against the rain and slipped out the door.

"WHERE DID YOU GET THIS?"

Aydin had returned with ends of sausage, heels of bread and a cold cooked turkey neck.

"That girl, the one who let me sleep in the root cellar. Summer, her name is." Aydin swallowed a mouthful of sausage and grinned. "She likes me. I promised we would play at her inn tonight though—you don't mind?"

Rowan shook his head, bemused. Who would have thought a rich merchant's son would be such an accomplished moocher?

At last Aydin was ready to get to work. "We'll have to play your Backender music, I suppose." He pulled his viol from the case and plucked at the strings to test their tuning.

Rowan busied himself with his own instrument, slipping on the shoulder strap and resting the box on his left knee before unhooking the bellows. He warmed up with a snatch of a simple jig, deliberately picking one of the tunes Aydin had butchered in the market the day before.

Check it out, smart-arse, he thought, as his fingertips skipped over the buttons. Just a couple of lines, before moving on to arpeggios to stretch out his fingers. He looked up to find Aydin staring at him.

"That's…What were you playing there?"

"We call those arpeggios." Rowan smiled wickedly. It was nice to have the tables turned, if only for a moment.

"No, before—is that what I was playing?"

Rowan shook his head. "No, it's what you were *trying* to play. It's called 'The Cat and the Cream.'"

Aydin seemed oblivious to the dig, all business now. "Play it again," he commanded. Then, noticing Rowan's raised eyebrows, he added, "Please."

It was a tune Rowan hadn't played for years, except as a warm-up or when requested by an audience member. But his mother had taught him not to sneer at the old favorites. "It may be old and worn-out to you," she said, "but people in the country towns don't get to hear music every day. Why shouldn't they want to hear a tune they know and love?"

He played it with care, driving the rhythm along while flickering—light and precise—over the melody and trills. "Like a fairy dancing on the neck of a galloping horse," his dad used to say. And he took it fast, holding back just enough to keep the melody clear, his right knee jigging in time.

When Rowan was done, Aydin let out a long whistle of admiration. "I bought some music in Shiphaven," he said. "And I played it right, but it still sounded like crap. All the tunes did." He shrugged. "I thought you Backenders just had bad music."

It was an apology, of sorts. Now Rowan could afford to be gracious. "I'd probably murder your music, too, if I tried to play from a score without ever hearing it." He grinned. "Why don't you pull out whatever you bought, and we'll work on those tunes first?"

THE OWNER OF THE PIG'S EAR listened to Rowan's proposal with open skepticism. When Rowan wound to a halt, he tipped his grizzled chin toward Aydin. "'Twas you playing in the square yesterday." The chin moved skyward, revealing a pouched throat bristling with several days' growth of heavy beard. ("I thought he had a hedgehog nesting under there!" Aydin joked later.) While the man gave his stubble a slow, thorough scratch, apparently as a polite alternative to saying what he had thought of Aydin's playing, Rowan quickly pulled his box out of the case.

"Could I give you a sample, sir?" he asked.

The scratching stopped, and Rowan glimpsed the publican's tired eyes widening in surprise. The button box was a fairly new invention, and there were few with the know-how to make and set the delicate metal reeds and rows of horn buttons. They wouldn't see one often in the backcountry—and Rowan's was one of the best. More to the point for this demonstration, it was a beautiful instrument, inlaid on the ends with enamel and mother-of-pearl, the bellows made of supple black kidskin. Without waiting for permission, Rowan began a breakneck version of a popular reel. He wasn't a flashy-looking player—his father had told him more than once that he hunched over his box like a broody hen—but he didn't have to be. The box had enough flash for both of them.

"By the Blessed Brew! Now *that's* music!"

The old boy doesn't look so tired now, thought Rowan. In fact he was grinning from ear to ear. "I didn't expect that from a lad so young, and that's a fact." Young or old, it wouldn't be often that this town saw musicians as accomplished as Rowan. But in this case, being underestimated worked in his favor.

"There'll be plenty more tonight, and my partner here does a very good job of backing me up," Rowan assured him. He felt Aydin stiffen behind him at the slight, but it was clear that the publican's first impression of Aydin had not been good. Better to downplay his role.

"We'll play for your best dinner and a silver dallion each," Rowan offered.

"Dinner and a *half*-dallion apiece," countered the owner.

"For a half-dallion each, we'll play through the dinner rush," said Rowan. "Then you feed us. If there is enough of a crowd left afterward and you want us to continue, another half-dallion between us." He stuck out his hand. "Mister...?"

"Oh, just call me Burl." Burl sighed and brushed palms with Rowan. "If I'm going to be bleeding my life savings into your pockets, you'll hardly be calling me Mister." He pointed a stubby finger at the boys. "People will come early on account of the rain. Be here by five bells—and you'd better have more than that one tune."

They didn't have all that many more, Rowan reflected as they pelted back to the caravan under a cold driving rain. Aydin was a fast learner but easily distracted. They had less than one hour to cram a few more tunes. He hoped his new partner could beat a drum in time to the pieces he didn't know.

I'm having fun, Rowan realized with a jolt, as they dove into the caravan. The bargaining, the practicing, even the challenge of putting together a decent act at such short notice. For the first time since—Rowan rarely finished that phrase in his thoughts. *Since* had come to stand for just one event. But for the first time since, he actually cared about his craft. He would work hard tonight to make it a good show.

IN BED THAT NIGHT, Rowan for once felt truly relaxed— tired in a good way, from a long day's work. "Well fed, well paid and well played," his father used to say at the end of a day like this. The clenching knot in his belly that had become his constant companion had eased. The tension between himself and Aydin was also—for now—gone. They had done well together, Rowan even managing to drum up the crowd's interest in a few of Aydin's pieces by presenting his knowledge of "the exotic music of the Tarzine Lands" as a "rare treat" for their discerning ears.

Now, in the quiet darkness of the caravan, Rowan finally felt able to voice the questions that had been worrying him.

"Aydin." He blurted it out before he had a chance to change his mind. "About my sister…"

"Finally." Aydin's voice floated back to him from the back of the caravan. "I was beginning to think you would never speak of her."

"Do you still see her?"

"Yes, she's here. Not as clear as last night."

"Why is that—is she leaving?" Rowan didn't know if he would be relieved or sorry if Ettie left.

"I don't think so. We were sitting beside the stove that night—spirits are stronger around fire."

"Why?"

The covers rustled, and Rowan could picture Aydin's elaborate rippling shrug. "Who knows? Maybe the heat gives them energy."

"Aydin..." Rowan paused, trying to marshal his thoughts. What did he actually want to ask? "Why is she here?"

"How should I know? I don't talk to them, I just see them." The dismissive, almost contemptuous tone was back (*stupid Backender*), but Rowan made himself ignore it. This was too important to get sidetracked into an argument.

"Yes, but...how does she seem? I mean, does she look sad or in trouble, or what?" Something had kept her from moving on to the deadlands. Why hadn't she gone with his parents?

Aydin's voice softened. "I don't think so. They say the dead sometimes stay because they get lost and cannot find their way to the spirit world, and that others stay because of a great anger that holds them to the earth. I do not think either is true of your sister. She is not drifting about aimlessly—she stays very close to you. It's hard to see ghosts in bright daylight, but she came up very clear on our first meeting, when I tried to chase you out of the square. And she doesn't look angry. She looks—" There was a pause while Aydin considered. "She looks *watchful.*"

She's watching over me. The thought came to Rowan with a certainty that took his breath away. Hadn't she been like that in life, mending the rip in his shirt before their mother was even aware of it, slipping him the last honey cake from a pocket in her apron? Rowan was stricken with remorse at how little notice he'd taken of these gestures and how often he'd brushed off the little girl trailing behind him.

Oh, Ettie. The tears welled up and spilled down Rowan's cheeks when he tried to blink them away. She was here because of him, so he wouldn't be left alone. But she shouldn't have stayed. He was holding her to the earth when she should be resting in the peace of the dead-lands before entering her next life.

Snores broke the dark silence. Aydin or Wolf? He couldn't tell. Either way, Rowan found it comforting rather than annoying. It was nice not to be completely alone. And it was nice—he surprised himself with this thought—yes, it *was* nice to think that Ettie was nearby. All the guilt he felt about keeping her earthbound could not change that fact: it felt good to fall asleep in his chilly caravan thinking that his sister was, in some way, still in the bunk across from his.

EIGHT

Despite their late night, the boys had the mules harnessed and ready to go well before midmorning. It had been decided over dinner that they would travel together for a while.

"So you have plans?" Aydin had asked in his direct way. "Besides wandering around piss-pot towns in a caravan, I mean?"

"Of course I do." Rowan's voice was a little too vehement, mainly because, until very recently, he *hadn't* had any plans. He had not been able to think in terms of a future extending beyond the next couple of days. Not that it had taken much thinking—it was obvious what he should do.

"I need to get to Clifton, on the south coast, by the beginning of the Month of Rains. That's..." Rowan squinted across the smoky inn, trying in vain to figure it out.

"Well, I'm not sure exactly when that is. I've kind of lost track of time lately. But it's coming up soon."

Aydin raised his eyebrows in mock dismay. "Weeks of snow, and now we are in for rains?"

"I heard," said Rowan casually, "that half the Tarzine lands are desert, good for nothing but goats."

"And I heard," countered Aydin, "that the Backender old ones all have moss growing out their ears from the constant damp."

Prosper and the Tarzine Lands did have very different climates. The sprawling island they shared was defined by the looming cones of three large volcanoes that had burst out of the high mountain backbone of the island. Though they had not erupted in living memory, the land surrounding them was a dead black sea of hardened lava, a harsh no-man's-land that no one—neither Tarzine nor Prosperian—cared to cross. The prevailing winds swept across Prosper and foundered on the mountains, bringing rain and a rich silt of lava ash that made the country green and sometimes sodden. The land on the other side was warmer and drier, less fertile overall but able to grow some crops—grapes, for example— that couldn't survive Prosper's winter storms.

"And so, why this Clifton place? You have family there?" Just for a second, Rowan thought, Aydin looked wistful. The impression was fleeting, but it gave him a jolt. Even when Aydin had told his terrible story, Rowan had never really thought how frightening his friend's flight must have been, how lonely to be traveling a strange land with no word of his family. For all his haughty self-assurance, Aydin was adrift, just like Rowan.

Rowan shook his head. He could go to his Uncle Ward and Aunt Cardinal—he would *have* to go at some point, at least to pass on the news of what had happened—but he couldn't see himself staying at their rural home up in sheep country for long. He was almost sixteen, too old to depend on others for his livelihood, and certainly not about to trade in his music to work in his uncle's business, even if it were offered. That big room full of clacking looms and the store-front piled to the rafters with bolts of cloth was the last place he'd want to spend his days.

He shook his head again, this time to dispel that unwelcome vision. "No, Clifton is…well, it's like the center of all music." Aydin snorted, and Rowan corrected himself. "I mean all *Prosperian* music. The guildhall is there, and many of the best instrument makers, master teachers in every instrument…But mainly, every spring there is a great gathering of musicians. Musicians looking for hire, ensembles that need extra players, stewards whose lords are wanting music for a special occasion or house players for the year. You can sign up to play on the official showcase program, but there is also work everywhere. Many people come just to listen, so every inn and pub has music night and day. Even the street players do well."

Aydin was listening intently. "So you will go and find work, new people to play with?"

"I hope so, yes." Said bald like that, it made Rowan's stomach roil. He'd often played with different people for a few tunes or an evening, but to actually join up with strangers, live with them, travel with them—well, plenty of players did just that. He would just have to get used to it.

"It's a big place, this Clifton?" Aydin waved his hand back and forth. "Bigger than this, I mean?"

"Much bigger," Rowan assured him. "It pretty much doubles its population in the spring, but even through the year it's a good-sized town."

"And it's a harbor town, I suppose, being on the coast?"

"Uh-uh." Rowan shook his head, his mouth too full to speak. Piss-pot town or no, Burl's roast lamb was the best meal he'd had, well...since. He took his time swallowing, then shot Aydin a look. "Names mean something around here, remember? It's a cliff town. No harbor—just a sheer rock wall into the sea."

Aydin nodded thoughtfully. "It will suit me, I think, this Cliff-town."

THEY TRAVELED SOUTH into full spring. Rowan knew the weather was more or less the same all over Prosper, but it really seemed they were leaving the last of winter behind their wheels.

Within days, the nights were warm enough that they abandoned the smoky stove for open-air campfires and, when they weren't working, sat and watched the flames for hours. They talked (at Aydin's prodding) or played (at Rowan's urging) or simply sat, each wrapped in the private, drifting thoughts that fire always seemed to summon.

"Your sister likes our music, I think," Aydin remarked one night.

"Why? Is she here now?" Rowan tried to peer into the darkness beyond the fire without looking like he was trying to see her.

Aydin rolled his eyes. "Of course she is here. She is always here. When she disappears, I will tell you."

"So why do you think—?"

Aydin gestured at the air. Rowan squinted fiercely at the empty space, willing Ettie to appear.

"She is very clear by the fire here. But when we play, she becomes...brighter. Like a light was kindled inside her."

Rowan's throat tightened, and the tears welled up treacherously. Just when he thought he was getting used to the idea, could think of Ettie with a semblance of composure, something like this would undo him. It was as apt a description of Ettie's smile as he could wish for. She was— had been—an ordinary-looking girl, not destined for any great beauty, but when she smiled, she was transformed. *Like a light was kindled inside her.* It was a minute before he trusted himself to reply.

"She used to love to watch us play."

Aydin nodded. "And what did she play?"

"Ettie? Nothing." But not for lack of trying. That was a not-so-good family memory: Cashel's growing frustration with Ettie's lack of ability and her growing despair.

"She had..." *A tin ear. Wooden fingers.* "She just didn't have the gift, I guess."

Cashel had given her a high whistle for her seventh birthday—a compact instrument just right for small hands, and a good counterpoint to their mother's lower wood flute. And she had been so excited to learn...except she hadn't. Couldn't. Cashel and Hazel both taught her, and she practiced as diligently as Rowan ever had. Yet month after month, her whistle was shrill and off-key, her fingering slow, her rhythm jerky.

Gently, Hazel suggested Ettie try the fiddle. Maybe she just wasn't a mouth player.

Things were even worse with the fiddle. It set Cashel's teeth on edge to hear his own instrument tortured day after day, and his usual kindness became strained. By the time Ettie was nine and had been training for two years, the whole family began to dread her lessons. Cashel's corrections became more and more impatient, his (blatantly untrue) accusations that she was "simply not trying" more frequent, and the whole ordeal, more often than not, ended with Ettie sobbing on her bed.

Rowan had happened to overhear the conversation that finally put an end to it.

"I don't know what to do about her," his father was confessing, his voice distressed. "I can't be bullying her week after week like this. But Rowan at this age was already—"

"Leave her be, Cashel." Hazel had reached out her hand and laid it on her husband's wiry forearm. "You tried,

she tried. She's not a musician. Let her get on with her
life now."

"And what will that be, without the music?"

Hazel smiled, teasing now. "Why, I imagine she'll marry
some nice young man, raise his babies and work by his side.
She wouldn't be the first."

Cashel glowered and shook his head. "And if he dies,
or his business fails? She has nothing."

"Now, love." Rowan's mother was serious again,
her voice earnest. "Your sister had very bad luck, no one denies
it. But most young women are not left widows with two small
babies and a world of debt. On the other hand," she admitted,
"a market skill is a good thing to have. We might see about
apprenticing her with my brother when she's older. But
meanwhile, I need my baby for a few years yet!"

Aydin was Ettie's opposite, Rowan mused. The Tarzine
was undeniably musical. He was also lazy, uninterested in
expanding his repertoire despite Rowan's warnings that the
basic pieces they played now would be of little interest to
the Clifton crowd. Finally, when his languid shrug failed
to silence Rowan's nagging, he said tersely, "Music is your
job, not mine. I have other ideas."

NINE

The four men had been knocking on rooming-house doors and questioning Shiphaven's innkeepers for two days, and they were heartily sick of it—that much, they agreed upon. Even Jago would have to admit they had earned the mugs of ale lined up in front of them.

In the dockside area of the busy trading port, rough-looking men were common. But people instinctively gave these men a wide berth, and not because of their Tarzine clothes and accents. The knives hanging from their belts or strapped across their chests had something to do with it. But even without their weapons, they were unmistakeably dangerous. At the ale room where they drank now, the publican quietly refilled their empty mugs, hoping that if he didn't keep them waiting or make them come up to the taps to fetch the ale themselves like the other customers, there would be less chance of trouble.

One of the men, younger than the others, took a long swallow, belched and set his mug down loudly. "I say we call it quits," he argued. "We've looked at every bleeding lodging in the lower town. He's not here. And if he was, he's long since flown the coop. More likely he never stepped on board a ship."

"Be my guest." Voka had served Jago for years and knew exactly what happened to those who delivered half-efforts. "Tell you what, Jax, you go on back to the ship and tell the boss that you got tired of looking. I'm sure you'll get a handsome reward." Ragnar, another veteran, lithe as a cat and studded with gold, sniggered into his beer.

"Be more pleasant to pull out your own teeth," he advised.

"Fine." Jax bent his head and spiraled his fingers elegantly from his brow in a sarcastic, elaborate salute. "What do you suggest then? We've been everywhere."

Ragnar shook his head. "Not nearly everywhere. We've checked the docks, where the sailors and workingmen stay. But now I'm thinking—he's a rich boy, yeah? Used to the gen-teel life. So maybe he'll get out of lower town, head for a nicer neighborhood where he feels safer. What's a few more coins to him?" He looked round the table at his mates. Tyhr, never a man for words, nodded his head in agreement. Voka followed suit. But none of them were exactly thrilled at the prospect of another long day questioning landlords.

"HOLD ON TO YOUR WATER—I'm coming!" The Widow Broadbeam was as ample as her name, and it had been years since she had run down the two flights of stairs in her lodging house. She wasn't about to start now, especially for anyone rude enough to pound nonstop on her front door.

The minute she laid eyes on the men—her fleeting impressions began with *large, menacing*...progressed to *tattooed, bejeweled* (Gods above, was that a nose ring on the one?)... and finally registered *armed*—she knew they were trouble. "Sorry lads, full up," she said firmly and closed the door.

Or tried to close the door. Fast as a snake strike, the nearest man—the big one with the tattooed, shaven head and copper skin—had his shoulder through the jamb.

"Now, now, mistress, not so fast. We are just wanting nice talk." The voice was heavily accented but understandable enough. With one smooth movement, he thrust the door open and sent Missus Broadbeam staggering backward. Then all four came barging in, closing the door firmly behind them.

She was afraid now. She was alone in the house, the roomers out about their business, and these Tarzine men meant no good.

"There's nought here to steal," she gabbled. "Only the few coins in my strongbox, which you're welcome to."

"Peace, mistress." The bald man again. He must be the leader, or maybe the only one who could speak Prosperian. "We have no need for Backender coins! I say we are here for talk."

Missus Broadbeam eyed them cautiously. For all their rough air, they were well, if gaudily, dressed, and their gold rings looked real enough. "Talk about what?" she ventured.

"We look for young man. He is brother of Jax, here"— he gestured to a slim man with hawklike features, who gave her a predatory grin—"but is lost. Perhaps you have seen him?"

She was already shaking her head in denial. She knew who they were talking about all right—that nice boy Samik. May the gods preserve him from men such as this! "I haven't seen nobody like that," she proclaimed.

The bald man smiled patiently, but his eyes were suddenly sharp. "But I have not told how he looks: tall, thin, with long hair, nearly white. Very pretty hair. You remember his hair?"

She shook her head again, and suddenly he was beside her, his arm hard as a tree trunk across her chest, his knife pressing under her jaw. She gave out a squawk of terror. She hadn't even seen him move, he was that fast. "Please don't hurt me! Please! I haven't seen him, that's all."

"I think you did, mistress." His voice was very quiet, the menace thick. "I think you need help with memory." He nodded to his men, and her tidy entry room erupted in a frenzy of destruction. She cried out as one man pulled out his knife and ripped her prized tapestry into ribbons, and again as her lovely stained glass window shattered with a tinkling crash.

The men stopped abruptly, and Missus Broadbeam felt the knife press into her skin. She was trembling now, moaning with fear, and the foreign voice bored into her head. "Now. Next I use knife to help memory. This boy, you have seen?"

She was too scared to stay silent. These men, they would ruin her house, leave her impoverished, hurt her, maybe kill her. And Samik must be away safe by now.

"He was here," she cried. "He was here, but he's gone."

"Good." The knife eased away from her throat, just a bit. "Gone where, and when?"

"Weeks now," she exaggerated. "He just stayed a few days and then left. He didn't say where."

"Is shame." The knife pressed against her again, and Missus Broadbeam cried out as the sharp blade nicked at her skin. "Is not so much help. You must do better."

"He didn't say where," she cried. "Just—inland."

"So he goes on main road—your Western Carriageway?" The man's voice sharpened with interest, and she thought, for one fleeting, brave moment, that she would agree and send them that way. But in that moment of hesitation, the knife pressed hard again and fear opened her mouth. "Not that way," she sobbed. "He wanted to go through the backcountry."

The men conferred in their Tarzine gabble, but the knife stayed firmly in place. "Please," she begged. "That's all I know. I swear it, that's everything." She screwed her eyes shut, waiting for the next threat or cut. *May the gods forgive me if I've done harm to that boy*. But surely all she had told them was harmless—Samik could be anywhere by now.

The men seemed to have come to a conclusion. With one catlike motion, the bald man released her, sheathed his knife and joined his men as they trooped out the door. He turned back at the threshold and smiled in false apology. "One thousand thanks for your kind help. We regret your window."

BACK IN THE ALE ROOM, Ragnar bent over the map.

"You can't be serious," Jax protested. "We can't search the whole Backend interior!"

"We won't have to—look at this." Ragnar traced the roads with his finger. "Besides the Western Carriageway, there are three roads out of Shiphaven. Two are basically coast roads. Only one heads inland."

He cocked his head, considering. "Like I said before, our young buck's not used to living rough. He won't be wanting to sleep in a ditch, I'll warrant. So we're looking for a town within a day's journey, say about...here." The finger tapped the map, and they all peered at the spot.

"Greenway," Ragnar announced. "I'd wager we'll pick up his trail in Greenway. There, or the next town down the road." He looked around the table. "We need horses. I'll go report back to Jago. You lot, find us something decent to ride. Just buy them, clean and aboveboard. Meet me at the docks."

IN THE DEEP SILENCE OF PREDAWN, Samik sat up in bed. The cold air on his shoulders was like a slap in the face, but at least it brought him fully awake. The dream was vivid in his memory as though it were painted onto the inky blackness in the caravan. There was no action, just the single image: a dark night, a vast sky studded with stars, and the dim outline of two figures. Though he couldn't make out their features, he knew the slighter figure was Rowan. Of the other figure, the one who held Rowan close in a pinion grip, Samik could see only two things: the glint of his sword, and the faint reflection of light—starlight? torchlight?—off his bald head.

Was it a true dream, or just the meaningless weavings of his own sleeping mind? He couldn't tell. Samik shook his head, trying to clear it. The clarity, the realism, felt true. But it was easy to see how his own worry could have shaped it—here he was in a strange land, fearful of pursuit, traveling lonely roads with a stranger. It wasn't much of a leap from there to imagining Rowan in danger. The dream could even be his own conscience talking, warning him not to mix Rowan up in his troubles. Or it could be a true vision of the future, or a possible future. Dreams, even true dreams, were often more confusing than helpful.

His grandmother would have known how to sort it out. Samik felt a stab of loneliness—for his granny, who had died the previous winter after a long illness that shrank her to the size of a child—and then for his home and family. If only he knew how things were with them. But the Sight was like that; it didn't necessarily show you what you wanted or needed to know. His granny had taught him that.

She had it too, the Sight. His mother did not like to talk about it—that was a lot less puzzling, now that he had met Rowan. The Tarzines, however, did not see it as anything so remarkable: an unusual ability, yes, like being double-jointed, and not often any more useful.

There would be no going back to sleep, not for a while anyway. Samik felt for the little lamp clipped by his bed and the spark striker stashed beside it, and soon a tiny but comforting light flickered beside his head. He eased from the bed and groped below it until he found the pen, ink and account book his father had tucked into his pack.

He shrugged into his coat and propped the book against his raised knees, stashed the little inkpot on the ledge of the caravan wall and began to write:

To Father, Mother, Merik and Aunt Kir, regards from Prosper.

I don't know when or how I will find a way to send word to you, but I will write this anyway.

First off, I am well and safe, and hope you are too, especially Merik. I pray to the Mother of All that he has recovered and is no worse for wear, and that you are all safe. I have not seen anything resembling a temple since I arrived here, just sometimes a little outdoor shrine to an unknown Backender god, but I watch for a place to pledge an offering to the gods for your protection.

I'm afraid I have used up the money you gave me. But I have met up with a boy who also travels alone, a musician. He's not the best company—too serious and silent to be much fun.

Samik paused, thinking about the strange boy he'd taken up with. So often he seemed nervous and broody, with that distracting twitch in his right eye, a repetitive fleeting half-blink. But all that melted away when he played his box, as if he threw off a load of cares just by strapping it on. When playing, Rowan was confident and cheerful, his smile so wide and unguarded that you couldn't help but return it. And he was good, bringing even the mathematical, boxed-in patterns of Backender music to life.

But he's been very generous, giving me shelter in his caravan, teaching me to play Prosperian tunes and sharing any work and earnings we pick up. Also, he's had troubles of his own that no doubt dampen his spirits. We are traveling together to a music festival, where I hope to find a better living and, who knows, perhaps even a way of sending this message.

Until then, I send my love and wait for the day I can rejoin you.
Samik
P.S. So far, the wine here ranges from nonexistent to abysmal.

TEN

Rowan's course, plotted day by day from his father's hand-drawn map, had taken them meandering southwest along minor roads and through minor towns. At last, six days after setting out, they joined up with the Western Carriageway heading into Miller's Falls. Here, he had decided, they would spend a few days—and some of his precious stash of money. Thinking about the Clifton festival had made him realize how rough he had been living. His clothes were grimy, his hair an overgrown tangle. It would be an expensive stay—for starters, there'd be no camping at the edge of the market square in this size of town. He'd have to pay to park the caravan and stable the mules. But it was worth it. He was a musician for hire, and he would hurt his own cause if he auditioned looking like an unwashed beggar boy.

Aydin's eyes lit up as they entered Miller's Falls.

"My arse!" he marveled. "Don't tell me it's an actual city! I was beginning to think you didn't have any."

Rowan grinned. Aydin still irritated him—just days ago they'd had a testy confrontation about Aydin's tendency to leave all the chores to Rowan, as though he were the guest at some grand manor and Rowan his personal manservant. But Rowan had got used to his new friend's sense of humor, or perhaps had begun to regain his own. Either way, he was no longer so prickly about every imagined slight.

Miller's Falls had a proper merchants' quarter bordered by a long service lane, where anything from harness mending to laundry could be purchased. Their only difficulty was with the logistics: bath first, only to climb back into their grubby clothes? Or laundry first, with an overnight wait on the bath while the clothes dried? Aydin solved the problem. "You need new clothes to perform anyway, no?" Rowan hadn't really planned on new clothes, but once mentioned, it did seem reasonable. He had a chest full of clothes back at Five Oaks, but after months of hard wear, those he had in the caravan, even cleaned and mended, were barely presentable.

So that was it. They trooped into several tailor shops, grubby as they were, in search of suitable, ready-made clothes in their size. Rowan was lucky—of average height and build, he was a decent fit for some of the samples hanging in the shops. Aydin's tall, slight frame was a challenge, and so was his taste for extravagant colors and textiles beyond the reach of the bit of money he had saved since teaming up with Rowan. But in the end, he found trousers that, while too short, didn't fall off his slim hips, and an unhemmed shirt. Extra-long cuffs, hurriedly attached, finished the shirt, and he decided to simply tuck the pants into his high boots.

Armed with fresh clothing, they made their way to the bathhouse.

Aydin was squeamish about the public baths, and especially the oversized wooden half-barrels that served as tubs. "Gods, they look slimy. Do they clean these ever? We should have stayed at a proper inn, had a proper bath drawn in a proper copper tub. How clean can you get, sharing the scum of the unwashed millions?"

Rowan was unmoved. "You're one of the unwashed millions too, my friend. We'll leave more scum behind than the last five men combined. But you want an inn, go right ahead. I'm not keeping you." After months of dabbing at himself from a bucket of cold water, he was in no mood to be picky. He sank into the hot water, scrubbed every inch of his body with the grainy soap provided, and emerged feeling like a new man.

The shops were starting to close as Rowan hurried to his last errand. He ordered a mattress with straw stuffing, and then, in a moment of largesse, a second for Aydin. He had eaten alarmingly into his savings, but he also felt he had in some way returned to the world. If he ran out of money, well, he would just have to make more. It was time to stop pretending to live, and really do it.

Brave words—but even as he said them firmly to himself, a part of him wanted to cling to his grief, hide in his caravan and never come out.

"Oh, Ettie," he whispered. "I wish you were here to help me."

Maybe she thinks she is. Maybe that's why she's staying, because of wishes like that. Rowan glanced around and saw, as always, no sign of her. Still he made himself say the words out loud, no matter how foolish it felt: "Don't worry, Ettie. I know what to do now. I'll be all right."

A part of him—the other part, the part that made plans and bought new clothes—even believed it.

ON THEIR SECOND DAY in Miller's Falls, Rowan found a decent corner for busking. As he had predicted, the towns-folk had little time for the tired old tunes that made up most of Aydin's repertoire—living so close to Clifton, their musical tastes were much more discerning. On the other hand, his Tarzine music did catch their interest, so the boys mostly took it in turn to back each other up on the drum and let each shine at what he did best.

On the third day, at dusk, they got hired by the barkeep from an inn a few doors down from their post.

"You two looking for work?" They had barely finished their tune when he barked out the question. Rowan looked him over: a thin, harried-looking man, eyebrows pulled together in a frown. In a hurry, by the looks of things. That was fine with Rowan.

"Definitely."

"Good. Bonehead who was supposed to play drank himself blind, fell down the bloody stairs and broke his arm. Meanwhile we've got half the town showin' up to drink the health of the mayor's son what got married. They'll be expecting entertainment!"

"No worries, sir," said Rowan. "We'll be there."

"Six bells. Don't be late," the barkeep charged with a pointed finger. "Or drunk!"

He had disappeared behind the black, iron-strapped door of the inn before Rowan realized his mistake and let out a groan.

"What?"

"We didn't talk money. We don't even know what he's offering."

"No matter." Aydin rippled his shoulders in that elaborate shrug. "If it's inside and there's drink to be had, it will be better than this."

SAMIK DIDN'T MAKE IT back to the caravan that night.

A noisy table of young men called them over during their break. "Great music, you lads are just great," slurred one, already drunk. "Sit down, have a drink!" He motioned to his fellows to pass up the jar they were sharing.

"No thanks," Rowan smiled, polite but already easing away. "I never drink while playing." Typical. Careful, cautious Rowan. Samik suddenly realized how fettered-in his weeks in Prosper had been. He grinned his thanks, grabbed the mug that was offered and sat himself down.

"Thanks, don't mind if I do!" He raised his mug to cheers all round and downed it quickly. His seatmate pounded his back enthusiastically. "Another for our friend, here!"

"By all means, but I'll have to go slow with this one," he warned. "I still need to be able to play."

"Join us after," his seatmate offered. "We'll be carousing all night."

Samik considered the young man: brown hair, blue eyes, nice open grin.

"I'm Heath." Heath gestured around the table. "That's Brook, and Toby, and Flint, and…" Samik lost track after that—so many quaint Backender names.

"Aydin." He raised his mug again. "And yes, I'd like that."

The table was even rowdier by the end of the night, but no one had become belligerent or sick—a good sign. They all made a show of pushing around to make room for him, filling his mug to overflowing. Once again, he found himself beside Heath, who slung an arm across his back in welcome.

As Samik looked up from his mug, Rowan caught his eye. He was standing a few feet away, clearly impatient to get home.

"You go ahead. I'll catch up with you later," Samik said. Rowan looked stung, and Samik felt a twinge of regret, but Kiar's Great Ax, there was more to life than working and sleeping. Samik was overdue for some fun, and if Rowan wasn't the fun type, well, he would have to find his way home alone like a big boy.

As for Samik, he would just go where the night led.

EVERY STEP OF THE WALK HOME the next morning was painful, but Samik was content.

He hauled himself up the steps of the caravan, fell into the chair at the little table and buried his face in his hands with a groan.

"Mother Muki save me, my head."

"What happened? What's wrong?" Rowan's voice was sharp. He stood in the galley, his hands dripping from washing up.

Samik winced. "Your voice is too loud, that's what wrong. I'm fine. Just royally hungover." Then he grinned. "Ahh, but it was worth it. At least, I think it was. I'm not sure I remember all of it. God's teeth, it's been a long time since I had an adventure."

Rowan rounded on him. "You could have told me you weren't coming home! Do you have any idea how worried I was? I was out with Wolf at dawn, looking for you."

Samik cast a pale eye his way. "Who asked you to? What are you, my mother?" A huge yawn overtook him—his bunk beckoned. He heaved himself up from the chair. "I hope you've done your practicing already. I'm going to bed for a bit."

"Not for long, you're not," Rowan snapped. "We're leaving today."

"What? You can't be serious," Samik protested. "We've barely arrived."

"Every night here costs me money. And I need to get to Clifton."

Or punish me for my night on the town, Samik thought. A day in a lurching cart would do nothing for his queasy stomach. "What about your mattresses?"

"I'll pick them up now. Enjoy your nap." And Rowan strode out the door, opening it all the way for a nice prolonged screech and letting it slam behind him.

ROWAN'S RESENTMENT still simmered as he struggled to maneuver the mules, each with a mattress slung over her back, through the narrow streets. Aydin should be helping him do this, he thought, not lying around uselessly, moaning about his head. Had he even thanked Rowan for the mattress? Rowan didn't think so. The fact that his difficulty was partly the result of his own poor planning—he should, he now realized, have hitched up the mules and taken the caravan to pick up the mattresses on their way out of town—did not put him in a better mood.

He felt like a fool, remembering how alarmed he had been when he woke up and realized Aydin had not returned. He had roamed the narrow, shadowed streets picturing Aydin ambushed by the warlord's men, dragged into an alleyway behind the buildings, his body hidden among the heaps of trash. When instead—

His thoughts were interrupted when he met a farmer pulling a load of produce in a handcart, and he had to wrangle the mules into single file to allow him to pass.

When he reached the sign of the Boar's Head Inn, Rowan led the mules into the courtyard where he had paid to park the caravan. Wolf, sprawled in a patch of sun in front of the door, thumped his tail at Rowan but didn't bother getting up.

Leaving the mules untied, Rowan pulled open the door and stuck his head inside.

"Aydin—give me a hand with these."

Silence.

With an irritated sigh, Rowan strode down to Aydin's bed, intending to roust him out—but the bed was empty. The caravan was empty. He went back to the courtyard and scanned the yard, taking in the parking area, the stables, and the inn itself. Surely he wasn't in there, drinking again?

Wolf got up suddenly and trotted around the side of the caravan. He probably just had to pee, but when Rowan heard the dog whine, he followed. And there was Aydin, standing stock still, ignoring Wolf's nudges.

"Aydin! What are you doing there?"

It was as if he hadn't spoken. Aydin didn't so much as twitch in reply. Worried now, on top of annoyed—with Aydin it was sometimes hard to tell which emotion won out— Rowan strode over and planted himself in front of the Tarzine.

"What in—?" Now he was well and truly spooked. Aydin's eyes didn't flicker from the spot they were trained on, nor did his expression change. He genuinely appeared not to see or hear Rowan. Wolf pressed his nose against his master again with a plaintive, worried whine.

Rowan pivoted and stared in the direction Aydin was focused on. He saw some scrubby shrubs, another caravan. No Tarzine warlords, or anything else that could explain Aydin's behavior.

"Merik is alive."

Rowan whirled back. Aydin's face was bright with relief and joy. His hand absently stroked Wolf's gray head as the dog leaned against him.

"What? That's great! Did you get a letter or something?" Even as he said it, Rowan realized it didn't make any sense. Or if it did, it meant someone knew where Aydin was, which was not great, not at all.

"No." Aydin shook his head serenely, composed once more. "I saw him. He was sitting up eating something—soup, I think." For the first time he looked directly at Rowan, his smile mischievous. "Of course I don't know for sure that he is entirely all right, but he can at least feed himself as greedily as ever."

Confusion, disbelief, anger at being the butt of a prank—it all came roiling back, just like the night Aydin had first mentioned Ettie. If this was a hoax—and it must be—then Ettie's ghost was a hoax. Rowan was just a hick Backender, an easy mark, and Aydin was playing him. Well, he'd had enough.

"You're brother's dead, then," Rowan said flatly, and was ashamed at the mean flush of victory he felt when Aydin's smile faltered and his face drained of color.

"You have news?" Aydin whispered.

"I thought you saw ghosts," Rowan snapped. "Dead people. If that's true, then you must be seeing the ghost of your brother." He turned on his heel, suddenly wanting only to get away from Aydin. "Heska's teeth! I'm tired of being the butt of your sick joke."

Aydin's blow clipped the back of his head and made him stagger to keep his balance. By the time he found his feet and turned, fists raised, he and Aydin were a few paces apart. Just as well. The sight of the tall boy's face—white and set, livid spots of color high on his cheekbones, the eyes cold and hostile—gave him pause.

"Ignorant Backender filth! You tell me my brother is dead and say *I* make sick jokes! I should beat you bloody for that."

Rowan's anger evaporated when he realized what he had done. He felt sick with shame.

"I—" Rowan twitched open his hands, struggling to fish out even a few of the words that had apparently crammed into his throat and wedged there too tight to dislodge. "I thought—" He slumped in defeat.

"So you don't understand something, you assume it's an attack on you. It's nothing to do with you. I see ghosts. Sometimes I see other things. Believe me or not—I don't give a crap."

5

With an air of wounded dignity, Aydin called Wolf back to his side and yanked open the caravan door. Rowan flinched at the long screech and the slam as it hid both from sight.

Miserably, not knowing what else to do, he unloaded the mattresses and set to harnessing the mules. He would have to bring the mattresses into the caravan before they left—but right now he didn't have the nerve to face Aydin. It was on Rowan to apologize, he knew that. He still could hardly believe what he had said. He had been thinking only of a way to fight back against what he assumed was a mean joke, had never dreamed Aydin would take him seriously. But that was no excuse. Now he would have to find the words to make it right.

ELEVEN

Not that way.

On the second day out of Miller's Falls, Dusty and Daisy came to a halt before a fork in the road. The main way was clear—they were on an actual road now, not the narrow country lanes they had traveled in the backcountry. Rowan pulled the left reins to turn the mules away from the narrow side road branching off to the right and clucked at them to walk on.

And then...Had he really heard that voice? He'd heard it before; he didn't doubt that now. But...

Rowan hesitated, peering down the side road. The vegetation was thick and overgrown, the trees arching over the lane to form a green, shadowy tunnel. *Are there no robbers in Prosper?* Aydin's earlier question came back to him. The Tarzine had been amazed at the dense woodland that sometimes came up to the very edge of the back roads. "In my country—well, except maybe for the badlands—this would be cleared back a bow's length to prevent ambushes," he had said. Rowan shrugged. He wasn't worried about being robbed, not on lonely roads anyway. In the cities, where thieves clever at picking pockets and locks congregated, more care was needed. Still, the taboo against stealing the tools of a craftsman's trade was very strong, even if people no longer believed quite so fervently in the guild god's curse, and most of what Rowan owned was his instruments.

No, highwaymen didn't worry him. But the side road would be a detour at best, more likely a dead end petering out into nothing at the last farm or a lake edge. He turned back to the main road.

Not that way.

With a muttered curse, Rowan pulled up the mules, then turned and clambered under the canvas flap into the caravan. Grabbing the map, he spread it out on the little galley table.

"What is it?"

Aydin, up on one elbow in his bunk, his white-blond hair a matted tangle from sleep, eyed him blearily. It was an advantage of Rowan's curls—or as Aydin put it, the *one* advantage—you couldn't tell if they were tangled or not.

"I'm just checking the route," said Rowan. With his finger, he traced the road from Miller's Falls and had just found what must be their turnoff when Aydin loomed over his shoulder.

"I thought it was clear—the main road all the way."

Rowan hunched his shoulders in annoyance. For once he wished Aydin had just stayed in bed. After their Big Fight— Rowan thought of it that way—Aydin had accepted his mumbled apology with surprising good grace, after extracting in payment an extra day in Miller's Falls to sleep off his bad head. But to Rowan the truce still felt fragile, and he was not keen to get into another argument. "It is. I just…I just think maybe we should take this other route." It was, in fact, a detour, looping around through a number of villages and rejoining the Western Carriageway below the Gull River.

Aydin poked his head out the front flap and then climbed right through. Rowan sighed and followed to find Aydin standing in the roadway, looking incredulously at the dark side road.

"There? You want to go down there? We are finally on a nice smooth road, passing through nice civilized towns and you want to drag us back into the bush?"

Rowan colored. He had been going to tell Aydin about the voice he heard—or thought he heard. He had thought maybe Aydin of all people would give it credence. But faced with such scorn, he couldn't.

"The mules didn't want to go," he muttered, defensive now. "Sometimes they know—"

"The mules. I see. That would be the same mules that didn't want to go into the stable where a soft bed and big meal awaited them? The mules you had to drag away from the gripeweed they were determined to poison themselves with?"

Rowan stood glowering and tongue-tied, unable to counter Aydin's ridicule. When he saw Aydin's mouth open for another volley, he gave up.

"Forget it. It was just an idea."

He picked up the reins and smacked them against the dusty flanks of the mules with a loud "HO!" Startled by the sudden action, they set off smartly down the road, the caravan following with a lurch.

"Bloody—" Aydin had to scramble up beside him to avoid being left behind.

BY LATE AFTERNOON they were nearing the river, and the mules were throwing up clods of mud instead of dust. There had been rain in these parts and plenty of it. Rowan had watched the hard-baked road become first damp, then slick and pocked with puddles. It was perfectly passable though, and it looked like the rain was done—the sky was bright, with only a few lingering clouds. They should easily make the town of Gull Crossing, just on the other side of the bridge, well before nightfall.

Rowan let his mind drift to the clop of hooves and the joggle of the caravan. There'd be no more anonymity once they got to Clifton. There would be people he knew, long-time friends and rivals of his parents. He'd have to go to the guild and report their deaths, register as a performer... and tell what happened over and over again. He wondered who he might run into, who he might find to play with.

He tried not to think about the possibility that nobody would offer him a place.

The mules stopped again. Rowan looked up to see the Gull River glittering before him at the foot of a steep hill. The bridge was some way to their right, for the road had been cut diagonally down the bank to ease the pitch of the descent. It was muddy but not washed out, and Rowan wouldn't have given it a second thought if not for that voice he had heard. As it was, he climbed down and gave the mules' harness fastenings a thorough check, making especially sure that the shafts were secured so there was no chance of the wagon overtaking the mules on the hill.

Of course, Aydin poked his head out.

"What now?"

"Nothing," Rowan said shortly. "Routine check before a hill. Go back to your beauty sleep, why don't you?" He felt himself color, embarrassed by his own hostility. It was pathetic how easily the Tarzine could get under his skin, how sensitive Rowan could be to any hint of ridicule.

And amazing how impervious Aydin was. Deliberately not taking the hint, he climbed through, instead, to the driver's bench.

"Why didn't you tell me it was such a fine day? Look at that river—don't you just love when the sunshine makes little diamonds all over the water? It's really a very pretty view."

Gritting his teeth, Rowan checked Daisy's belly band and then climbed up beside Aydin and gathered up the reins.

They took it slow, Rowan doing his best to avoid the wheel ruts carved into the mud by the day's traffic. The mules were steady, and Rowan had just mentally relaxed when it all fell apart.

Dusty's back foot skidded in the mud, and she stumbled and danced to regain her purchase on the slippery surface. Daisy—startled by the commotion, or maybe just misunderstanding the pull from her partner and trying to keep up—kicked into a trot. Dusty, still not steady on her feet and now being dragged forward, got her front foot in a pothole and lurched forward. And then they were out of control, the mules scared and running hard to get away, the caravan swaying and bouncing behind, too fast.

Aydin shouted out in alarm and then yelled in Rowan's ear, "Do something!"

"Take these!" Rowan shoved the reins into Aydin's hands. "Pull steady, not too hard." He groped at his feet for the brake lever, found it and pulled up.

"Not all the way," he remembered his father coaching. "Just till you feel the drag. Otherwise you could flip the whole works."

He felt the metal prong make contact with the wheel rim. It made a god-awful screech, but as he pulled harder, he could feel the drag on the caravan. He hung on, fighting the buck of the wagon.

"It's working!" Aydin's voice was a hoarse gasp in Rowan's ear. But he was right, the mules had stopped their panicky run and slowed to a trot. Ears twitching madly, flanks alive with shivers, they were still spooked but back under control. Maybe the more familiar feeling of the wagon pulling against them instead of pushing them forward had calmed them. Rowan looked ahead and saw that, although it seemed like they'd been careening down the hill for a lifetime, they had not yet reached its foot. He sent up a prayer to the god of travelers. They would not hurtle into the river after all. He was shaky with relief, barely able to keep his hold on the brake.

He looked again. They were way over at the edge of the road, the caravan's right wheels bouncing through grass and shrubbery.

"Aydin!" Crouched over the brake handle as he was, he had to crane his neck around to glimpse the tall boy's face. "Try to get them into the middle."

And then he was flying forward, pitched headfirst over the footboard and into a crazy jumble of mule legs. The crack of breaking wood rang in his ears and filled his thoughts. "A wheel. Cursit, CURSIT! Must have hit a rock. Gods' curse—we get this far and then break an almighty wheel?" Even as he thudded into the earth, tasting mud and feeling the wrench in his shoulder, his mind clung stupidly to the wheel.

"*ROWAN!*" Ettie's voice was a shrill alarm.

Rowan lifted his face from the mud and saw the blurred flash of a hoof inches from his face. The wagon had come to an abrupt stop, but the mules had reached their limit and were in a bucking, braying frenzy—and Rowan was about to have his head staved in. Scrambling backward, he made it under the shelter of the tilted wagon and just crouched there on his hands and knees. He'd had enough too. His breath came in tight little heaves, his throat somehow too narrow to let it through. His arms trembled under him, the pain in his shoulder sharpening into an insistent throbbing ache. He didn't even realize at first that he was crying.

And that's how Aydin found him—hiding under the caravan, sobbing like a little kid.

"Get out of there!"

The anger in Aydin's voice cut short the tears as sympathy never could. Startled, Rowan wiped his nose on his sleeve and glanced at the face framed in the opening between the wheels. Aydin's golden skin was blotched white and red, as though he had broken out in hives. He reminded Rowan of a squid he had once seen in a tide pool, the colors fading and blushing across its translucent body.

"Are you hurt?" Rowan asked as he clambered out from under the caravan.

"Yes, I am hurt." Aydin gestured to his pant leg, ripped and stained with blood on one thigh. He pushed Wolf's concerned nose away from it. "But you—you could have been killed!"

Was this how Tarzines showed concern? Rowan wondered. Aydin still seemed hopping mad.

Aydin came up and thrust his face inches from Rowan's, as he had on their very first meeting. The anger then had been largely fake, Rowan realized now. This time it was real.

"It was her, wasn't it?" Aydin accused.

"What...?" It was a feeble stall for time—Rowan knew who he was talking about—but it was all he could find to say.

"Your sister! It wasn't the bloody mules that made you hesitate at that fork, it was your sister!"

"How do you know?"

"She was bright as bloody day during that run down the hill, practically sitting on your head. Idiot! You get a warning from the dead, and you blabber on about mules? The demons take you! I should kick in your head myself!"

Aydin turned on his heel and stalked off to the mules. At least he had thought to tie the reins together and hitch them to a tree before ripping into Rowan.

TWELVE

Slowly, giving each other a wide berth, they took stock of the damage. Wolf was unharmed—he had been off the road investigating yet another enticing smell when they lost control. Aydin, who had always pleaded ignorance and left all mule care to Rowan, managed to get the mules calmed down and unhitched from their harness, and walked first Daisy and then Dusty up and down the road in front of the bridge, watching their gait carefully.

Rowan confirmed that the back right wheel was indeed ruined and saw with relief that the axle seemed undamaged. There was a spare wheel bolted to the bottom of the caravan, but he wasn't sure he could figure out how to change it. He wasn't sure his shoulder was up to the job either—he could almost feel it swelling up. He moved it gingerly in a little circle and grimaced. It hurt—really hurt. Not broken though, or he wouldn't be able to move it at all. Wasn't that right? He thought he'd heard something like that.

Aydin was on his way back to the caravan. Limping, Rowan noticed with a pang of guilt. *My fault.*

"My ma had some doctoring stuff in the caravan. I'll go get it."

"You might want to wash off first." Aydin spoke mildly, the anger faded to a kind of careful neutrality. "You're filthy."

Rowan was suddenly aware that he was coated in road mud—mud mixed with the excrement of every domestic animal that had ever been led or driven over the bridge. It was on his face, under his fingernails—and it stank.

Disgusted, Rowan hurried to the river, stripped off his boots and waded right in. It was shallow for a few steps and then dropped off, deep and cold. He sank under the icy water, scrubbing at his face, feeling the sting of the scrapes on his hands as his clothes billowed about him. When he surfaced, though, he realized his shoulder was too sore to swim properly. He made his way to shore with an awkward one-handed dog paddle, keeping his right arm tucked in close, and clambered out. He peeled off his pants, started on his shirt and realized that pulling it, wet and clinging, over his head was going to hurt like demons.

"Let me." Aydin maneuvered the loose tunic over Rowan's good arm and head, then drew it gently down his other arm.

"Thanks." Rowan gave a curt nod, somehow as discomfited by Aydin's moments of kindness as he was by his cutting tongue.

Aydin pushed a half-used cake of soap into Rowan's hand.

The awkward knot between them loosened, and Rowan grinned. "Best present I ever got." He waded back into the water and scrubbed.

"AT LEAST NEITHER OF THE MULES is lame," said Aydin. "That's amazing. Horses would have been hurt for sure."

"Would they?" Rowan didn't know much about horses, or mules for that matter. He broke more stale bread into his soup and chewed morosely. He didn't know much about wheels, either, and wasn't looking forward to facing that job.

The boys had smeared their various scrapes with the smelly ointment Rowan's mother had used for every childhood injury, wrapped Aydin's leg with a long strip of cloth cut from one of her skirts, fed and watered the mules and pulled together a meager supper, leaving the wheel for morning.

Aydin poured the last of the soup into his bowl and put the pot down for Wolf to lick. He stretched, belched and then pointed toward the river. Small shadowy forms flitted and swooped over the water.

"Bats spell bedtime. That's what my mother said when I was little. Anyway, there's not much else to do around here. I'm heading in."

"Yeah." Rowan stirred the last embers of the little camp-fire and carefully poured the water bucket over them. Steam rose with a satisfying hiss.

"Let's see," pondered Aydin. "Will I sleep with my head up or my head down?" The broken wheel had left the floor of the caravan distinctly tilted, especially at the back.

A puff of wind, the merest breath, lifted the hairs on the back of Rowan's neck.

"Take Ettie's bed," he said. "It will be a bit straighter."

IT WAS EASY ENOUGH TO UNBOLT the spare wheel and drag it out from under the caravan—though Aydin had to do most of the dragging, since Rowan could only heave with his left arm. The boys were debating the next chal-lenge—how to get the corner of the caravan raised so they could remove the broken wheel and slide on the new—when an elegant carriage pulled by a black horse with red fittings clattered down the road.

It came to a halt a short way past them, and a well-dressed man of about thirty hopped down.

"Trouble, lads?"

He had sized up the situation before they could reply. "Took the hill too fast, did you? Well, you're not the first. Need some help with that wheel?"

Rowan hesitated. In his experience, wealthy citizens didn't often go out of their way to help scruffy-looking young men, and that made him just a little cautious.

"That would be wonderful!" Aydin accepted for both of them. "We really have no idea what we're doing."

"My man's the carriage king." And soon the driver was stripping off his red jacket and eyeballing the wreckage.

"Where's your lift?" he asked.

"My lift?" Rowan didn't know what the man meant.

"Your lift, for cranking up the wagon."

"Ummm. I'm not sure if we have one," Rowan admitted.

The man, small, wiry and sharp-featured, shot him a look but said nothing. *Wondering if I stole it*, Rowan thought.

"Usually they're strapped under with the spare wheel," he said, and disappeared under the caravan, emerging triumphant a few minutes later.

As Rowan and the driver worked, the carriage owner and Aydin chatted like old buddies.

"Headed to Clifton?"

Aydin nodded in agreement.

"Musicians?"

"As a matter of fact, we are. Rowan there is the professional."

"Excellent, excellent." Their rescuer clapped his hands in approval. "The more, the better. I always do a fine trade during Festival, very fine indeed."

"And what business are you in, sir, if I may ask?"

"Oh, I buy and sell many things, you know." Aydin nodded as if he did actually know. "But most of my trade is in spirits."

At this, Rowan swiveled his head around to stare at the man, thinking he'd misheard through the noise of their work.

Spirits? But the man was miming taking a swig from a bottle. *Halfwit*, he thought. Of course he means *those* spirits.

"Ale, stout, whiskey. Mostly ale and stout during Festival. Musicians are a thirsty lot."

"Yes, certainly." Aydin's voice sounded different. Rowan was having a little trouble following the driver's instructions—*hold this steady, screw this in*—because Aydin's voice kept snagging his attention. He sounded older, smoother. More polite.

"Do you trade in wine at all?" Aydin's tone was casual, but Rowan could hear the subtle sharpening that betrayed his interest.

"A little. There's not much local call for it. Of course, the local product doesn't merit much call…" They drifted off toward the river, deep in conversation, and were soon out of earshot.

He didn't really mind that Aydin left him working alone in order to talk shop with a merchant twice his age. The carriage driver, despite his sharp manner, was a calm, steady worker and a willing teacher. When they were done, he wiped his hands on a cloth, shrugged into his uniform, and gave Rowan one last, valuable tip.

"When you get to Clifton, take your old wheel to Shale the wheelwright on Marketview Road—that's on the high side, mind. Tell him Purdy sent you. He's the best in town, and he'll give you a fair price."

THIRTEEN

Voka reined in at the top of the steep hill and surveyed the churned-up track leading to the river.

"We'll want to take this slow, boys. People have been having trouble with the grade, by the looks of it." Something big had ground deep ruts in the mud, veered right off the track, and left behind a large swath of bent and bruised shrubbery. Something—now that he thought of it—about the size of a caravan.

It hadn't taken them long to find the inn at Greenway where Samik had stayed. "Any idea where they were headed?" Voka had asked the barkeep. "There's a family emergency. His parents are most anxious to find the poor lad." At least that was what he tried to say; doubtless it was rougher around the edges in his imperfect Prosperian.

But this new story seemed to work. Either that, or the barkeep didn't really care.

EITHER WAY, THERE HAD BEEN no need for "persuasion." The man had readily volunteered, "He was asking round the tables for a ride south; picked up with a tradesman making deliveries." Still, they might well have lost Samik's trail if he hadn't joined up with that musician in Cedar Glen. The old geezer at the Pig's Ear had lit up when Voka described the boy. "Oh, sure, I remember him—tall, skinny beanpole of a fellow. He came in with that young box player—by the brew, that lad can play! Been a good long while since we've heard such music in these parts." He gave the stubble under his chin a fierce scratch and regarded Voka cautiously. Even alone and with his knives hidden, he was a man to treat with care. "He's no relation of yours, I suppose, so no offense, but the tall one didn't really seem to be able to keep up on that fiddle of his. I wondered why they were working together."

"They travel together, then?" Voka asked casually. He had learned something about these Backenders: he could intimidate them into talking easily enough, but they would often blab twice as much if he didn't alarm them.

The old publican was nodding. "It seems so. They'll be off to Clifton, I imagine, what with the Month of Rains just around the corner."

"The Month of...?" Voka wasn't following.

"You know, for the big festival. All the musicians go—leastways, those who don't have a permanent spot. Those lads have been living rough, by their looks—they'll be in Clifton, looking for work."

After that, it was simple. They cut straight west to the Western Carriageway and sent Jax, who had never ceased his complaining, back to Shiphaven to inform Jago, who waited with his ship at the docks. On horseback and traveling the main road, the remaining three would close a good chunk of the gap between them and the boys. By the time they arrived in Clifton, they should be right on their scrawny little heels.

"IS IT GOING TO RAIN like this every day?"

Samik stuck his head out from under the canvas flap and glared at Rowan.

"Don't blame me, I didn't order it!"

The rain had been steady all morning, gusting with the wind that blew off the ocean. There weren't many trees in this coast country to block rain or wind. *Maybe they'd all been blown down*, Samik thought.

"Well, is it?"

"Maybe most days, though not so hard." Rowan shrugged. "It *is* the Month of Rains."

Samik pulled the canvas tighter around his head and snorted. "So what genius decided to hold a music festival during the Month of Downpours? I thought you said there were street players and outdoor stages."

"The month before is too cold to camp," Rowan explained. "The month after is too late—people want to be settled by then, working through the summer season. They put up awnings and covered stages though."

"Oh, awnings. That's all right then. I'm sure they will keep us snug and dry." Samik offered his best sarcastic smile to Rowan's hunched back. This rain, blowing almost sideways at times on a heavy wind, would instantly drench anyone foolish enough to trust in an awning. Even the huge oilskin Rowan was wrapped in couldn't protect his exposed hands and hair.

"Just be glad we have a caravan to sleep in," said Rowan over his shoulder. "Some people camp."

Samik *was* glad to have a caravan and was about to retreat back into its relative comfort when Rowan called out, "Aydin, look at that!" He pulled up the mules and pointed.

From within his canvas kerchief, Samik peered through the rain.

"What? All I see are the same road and the same rain."

"There." Rowan pointed to the horizon. The road rose gently toward the coast, ending in a series of low, lumpy hills. "See on that middle hill? I'm pretty sure that's Clifton."

"Good. Giddy-up."

"Don't you want to ride up front and watch it come into view?"

"You must be mad," said Samik and closed the canvas gap firmly. There was no need for both of them to get wet. Besides, he was busy. An idea had come to him while he was talking to that merchant who stopped to help them with the wheel, and he needed some time alone to let it take root.

"I guess that's a no," said Rowan and started up the mules.

CLIFTON WAS BUSTLING, even in the late evening. The last rays of sun glinted off the limewashed buildings and made the wet cobblestones shine like polished tile. Rowan guided Dusty and Daisy slowly through the city. The rain had stopped and, to Samik's delight, the narrow streets were full of people. Here was a town where, even by Tarzine standards, people knew how to enjoy themselves. They threaded their way into the center of the city and then beyond, to the great field in the southeast quarter that was set aside for visiting players during the festival.

"The guild'll be closed by now," the porter at the gate had told them. "But the players' camp is manned all night. They'll give you one night free, even without the guild plaque, if you can convince them you're really musicians."

AT THE GUILDHALL the next morning, Rowan counted out the coins, trying not to think about how little remained of his money stash. Anyway he had no choice:

guild membership was a requirement for a spot on the showcase program, and Rowan needed to make himself visible as a player for hire.

Rowan's parents had bought him his own member-ship for the first time last year—a little rite of passage signifying that he had become a guild-quality musician, no longer riding on his parents' names. Though of course he had been, hadn't he? This year he wouldn't be the son who played so well for his age. He'd have to stand or fall on his own performance.

"Family name?" The clerk pushed his hair out of his eyes as he bent over the stack of parchments.

Rowan was relieved, really, that he and the young clerk didn't know each other. Simpler that way. "Redwing."

With a sigh, the clerk began burrowing through the papers to the Rs. "Outlier, Overhill, Peregrine, Ramsden. Right, here's Redwing...hmm."

Leaving a finger to mark his place in the stack, he craned his skinny neck around and peered accusingly at Rowan. "There are several Redwings here. Which one are you?"

"I'm Rowan." He tried to make his answer as clipped as the clerk's manner. *And please don't ask about the rest of us.*

He needn't have feared. Though barely past break-fast, the guildhall was already filling up with musicians, all needing something. The clerk had no time for pleasantries.

The clerk took his money, stamped his parchment with this year's seal, gave him his plaque and shouted "NEXT!" while shooing Rowan to move aside.

"Sorry, wait—I'm not done," he protested. This earned him another sigh, and a carefully neutral look that somehow made it plain just how much the clerk's patience was being tried. "I need to get on the showcase program."

The clerk's lips tightened in disapproval. "That's in the next room, toward the back. But you're late, you know. I doubt there is any space left."

Rowan found his way to a small room with large slates mounted against the wall, each detailing a different day of the showcase. A glance was enough to relieve Rowan's anxieties—today's slate looked full, but there were plenty of spots on other days. He pushed his way past the people milling about the slates and spoke to a motherly, bustling older woman who advised him on the best available time and signed him up without a single sigh or lecture. He emerged into the street slightly bemused by the whole experience.

"ROWAN! Oi, wait up, man!" The voice was loud as a town crier's and rumbled like a troll's. Not a second later, a heavy arm clapped across Rowan's back, making his sore shoulder flare in protest.

Timber. Rowan knew who it was without looking—there was no mistaking that booming voice. He felt his heart lift and sink at the same time, a sensation so odd that he actually clutched a hand to his chest as though to hold it together. The traitor tears burned behind his eyes as he turned. He blinked furiously, but there was no need. Timber's bear hug swallowed him whole, tears and all.

Timber had been his parents' best friend and musical rival for as long as Rowan could remember, and in some ways more of an uncle than his real one. Named "Timbre" in hopes that he would be blessed with a rich singing voice, he earned the nickname "Timber" in his teens by growing into a great slab of a man. "Tall as a tree and solid as a stump," he used to tell the kids with a wink when they were small, "and in my old age I'll be gnarled as a weepy willow."

Now as he unwrapped his big arms and held Rowan at arm's length—a ritual at every meeting, accompanied by the phrase, "Let's take a look at ye, see if you've matched my height yet"—his genial face fell into concern. "Oh now, lad, what is it?"

"Bad news, Timber," Rowan managed. "Can we go somewhere?" He desperately did not want to have this conversation on the street.

The older man didn't say another word, just draped his arm around Rowan's shoulders and steered him down the street. Though he must have been in an agony of impatience, he didn't mention the matter until they were ensconced in the empty back corner of a taproom with mugs of ale in front of them.

"I've never drunk ale right after breakfast," Rowan said. He wasn't sure he was going to like it either, not with his stomach already doing nervous flip-flops. But Timber took a long, sucking swallow of his and then set his mug down firmly.

"Now tell me."

It was the first time he had told someone who actually shared his loss. Timber's eyes screwed shut at the news, then his big freckled hand covered his face as his shoulders hunched in grief. There would be more conversations like this to come, Rowan thought bleakly. Worst of all would be telling his Aunt Cardinal and Uncle Ward. Yet there was comfort, too, in Timber's sorrow. That somebody else cared seemed to lift some of the burden of death from Rowan's shoulders.

Finally Timber straightened himself and took a deep, shaky breath.

"Ah, lad. I can't say how sorry..." He shrugged helplessly. "We heard there was plague at Five Oaks, of course, but everyone seemed to think you'd escaped it."

"Was it bad there?" It had been a long time since Rowan had had news of anyone, or anywhere. A long time since he'd cared to find out.

"Bad enough. The son died, and the earl's wife, and a fair number of servants. A handful of cases cropped up beyond the estate, and people were saying it would be the Death Years all over again. But it didn't keep spreading this time— it looks like it's died out. Now if it had been in a city like this one..." Timber shook his head in dread at the prospect. "Your dad did right to keep away from the settlements. Saved a lot of lives."

Rowan nodded numbly. A thought was trying to rise to the surface, and he was trying to keep it under the waves. It bubbled up anyway: Cashel hadn't done his family any good, cramming them together into a little caravan. Maybe their chances would have been better if they had stayed at Five Oaks.

He wondered if Pansy, the earl's daughter, had survived. He'd been giving her lessons for few months before they left. She was a beautiful girl, eyes as violet as her namesake, with a flirty way of teasing him that he was just starting to enjoy. "Mind you don't let her go beyond," his father had warned, and when Rowan grinned in reply, Cashel had become very serious. "I mean it, Rowan. It's a position of trust you've been given, and the earl will not tolerate a hired hand making free with his daughter. Not even if said hired hand is one of the blessed bards!"

"Rowan?" Timber's deep rumble brought his thoughts back to the present.

"Sorry, what did you say?" Timber's mug was already empty, and Rowan pushed his own across the table, glad of an excuse to be rid of it.

"I mean it. You're more'n welcome to stay with me, for as long as you'd like to."

"You wouldn't happen to need a box player?" A little flame of hope ignited in Rowan's chest. But Timber's face was already screwed into an apologetic grimace.

"I'm afraid not, lad. You know we have Bruin—he's twice your age and half the player, but Bryony would never sack him." Timber's ensemble wouldn't have been Rowan's first choice musically. They were known for their dance music, which meant lots of traveling in order to play repetitive figures for noisy, drunken, largely unappreciative crowds. But a year or two under Timber's protective wing would have made everything easier.

Instead, he shook his head quickly. "Then thanks, but no. I'm too old to mooch off you." He raised a hand against Timber's protests. "I know you don't see it that way. It's just that I need to be playing and earning my own way now."

Timber nodded his understanding. "You're scheduled for the showcase, I hope?" Rowan nodded. "Tell me what times, and I'll get the word out. I'll do what I can for you."

Rowan thanked him awkwardly and made to get up. "I should get going. I need to find a good busking spot, and you know how they fill up."

Timber stood with him and laid a restraining arm on Rowan's shoulder. "Are you all right for money, Rowan? Will the guild payment see you through?"

"The guild payment?"

"Aye, lad. For your parents…" Timber took in the confusion on Rowan's face and pulled him back down to the table. "Have you not reported their deaths yet?"

Rowan, not trusting himself to speak, just shook his head.

"I'll go with you now," declared Timber. "Your parents were guild members in good standing for many years. There's a death payment owing to you. It won't be much, but it will help." His full lips pressed together into a grim line. "As much as anything *can* help."

FOURTEEN

Now that he was about to step onto the stage, Rowan wished he had asked Aydin to back him up after all. Playing solo, with the stakes so high and before an audience that would neither stomp their feet and cheer in approval of your performance, nor hiss in displeasure, but rather silently appraise every ornament and error, was more nerve-racking than he had imagined.

The conversation with Aydin about the showcase had been an awkward dance of polite vagaries. Rowan, fairly sure but not certain that Aydin had no interest in seeking work as a player, and not wanting to insult or abandon him, had tried to suggest he was welcome to join in without making him feel obligated. Aydin, in turn, had acted like he didn't know what Rowan was getting at—or maybe, thought Rowan, he really didn't. It was easy to forget that Prosperian was not Aydin's—Samik's—first language. Finally, Aydin had asked, "What time is your showcase?" and when Rowan told him, said, "Then if you don't need me, I won't come. I have an appointment to keep."

So instead of being relieved that Aydin was not expecting to partner with him—honestly, he was more of a liability than an asset—Rowan felt absurdly disappointed that he would not be in the audience and hurt that he had not deigned to reveal what his "appointment" was about.

Now he took a deep breath and tried to let all that go. It was time to let go, too, of his doubts about his program. Most up-and-coming young players would lead off with something flashy played at breakneck speed—an attention grabber. Rowan, wanting to distinguish himself from the others, had decided instead on a sweet, lilting waltz. He had hoped it would suggest confidence and a more mature musical taste. The risk was it would, instead, suggest he couldn't play anything harder. He hoped he wouldn't lose his audience before the second selection, which would prove them wrong.

Let it go. It was all beyond his control now, all except one thing: playing the pieces as well as he could. He walked on stage, bowed to the unsmiling men sitting in the stuffy hall, and sat on the stool provided. As he arranged his box, he let his knee set the rhythm of the piece: *one,* two, three, *one,* two three, *dum* deedle deedle…

Heska save him, he'd been a fool. In his small caravan, beginning the piece with a single melody line and then building it gradually had seemed bold and lovely. But in the hall, the air seemed to swallow the thin notes before they even left the stage. *Just play, don't think.* The feeble single notes unreeled one after the other, agonizingly slowly, and finally Rowan found the music in them. The beauty of the melody came to him with an image— a memory—of Ettie, dancing with an imaginary partner as she hummed this lovely waltz. "Play it for me, Rowan," she had begged, and he had gone out to the green with her and played, and she had danced through the morning dew, barefoot in her nightie, the white fabric floating around her ankles...

When he was done, Rowan looked up, a little dazed, with really no idea if he had played well or not. His audience was still there, at least. He gave himself a mental shake and put his mind to his final selection, a tricky set of reels. There could be no wool-gathering on this one— it took every ounce of his skill and attention. *Not too fast,* he reminded himself. *Steady is more important than fast.* Still, he meant to take it both fast *and* steady.

At the end of the set, it was his mother's voice that guided him through. "Smile, dearie. It's a performance. Bow, don't bounce. Say 'Rowan Redwing' slowly in your head as you hold it. Don't bolt off the stage."

"Pretty waltz. What's it called?" asked the attendant who escorted him to an alcove just outside the hall.

"That's 'The Sun's Desire,'" said Rowan. He must have played it decently then, he told himself. Or maybe the fellow was just trying to put him at ease. He appreciated the comment, either way.

"Now don't feel badly if nobody comes to speak to you," continued the attendant. "No one gets job offers on the spot. If they're interested, they'll come to your second showcase, ask around..." He stopped in confusion. A half-dozen men and women, some of whom Rowan recognized, were lined up at the alcove, with more approaching.

"Huh. Unless, I guess, you're a brilliant young box player. Get in there now, and meet your adoring fans!" With a friendly push, the attendant left him to it.

But they weren't prospective employers. Timber had got the word out, and friends and colleagues of Rowan's parents were dropping by to give their condolences. As Rowan stood and endured the painful repetition of sympathy, he was genuinely moved that people had come. Up to now, his family's death had been so anonymous—as though they had never existed, except to him. But what if someone *did* want to speak to him about work and found him instead in the midst of—well—this?

A large woman Rowan had never met flung her arms around him and pressed his face into her impressive bosom. "You poor thing." Her loud, throaty voice resonated in his ears. "All alone in the world." A last clench, and she released him. "If you need someone to sing at the funeral rites, I'd be honored," she said. "When will you hold them?"

"I don't know," Rowan admitted. Funeral rites. Wasn't it too late for that? "I haven't really had a chance to think about it."

The woman shot him a strange look—not much wonder, given that he'd had nearly three months to think about it—and made way for the next person. "I'm Iris," she called over her shoulder. "Just ask around—you'll find me."

She looks like an Iris, thought Rowan. *Purple and overblown.*

SAMIK SAT ON THE FRONT STEP of the caravan, stretched his long legs out before him and tipped his head back into the sun. It was important to take full advantage of these rare interludes of sunshine; the constant damp was making him feel soggy, as though mushrooms might sprout up between his toes. He was pleasantly close to dozing off when Rowan returned, looking serious and preoccupied—as usual.

"So no work yet?"

Rowan shook his head. "Not even an inn or taproom—I think they were nearly all booked before we even arrived." He shrugged. "Hopefully my second showcase will help."

"You look like you could use some fortification," said Samik. "Come inside—you're just in time for tea." He pulled himself to his feet, pulled open the door and bowed grandly. He hadn't known if Rowan would return or not and had been about to enjoy his little feast alone, but this was better. He couldn't wait to see Rowan's reaction.

He wasn't disappointed. Rowan's eyes went round with surprise when he stepped into the caravan.

"What's all this?"

"This," said Samik, still with the grand manner, "is *real* food." He turned to the stove, where the water was boiling, and busied himself making proper tea. "I thought the pastries would do well for our tea. They're filled with berries and cream. But, as you can see, that's not all I have." He gestured toward the galley table, where meat pies, a wheel of cheese, fresh-baked bread and a dish Samik had never tried, made from eggs and new spinach wafted tantalizing smells into the air.

Rowan demolished one pastry and started on another before coming up for air.

"How did you buy all this?" he demanded.

"I went busking today, as you suggested." Samik flashed him a sly grin.

"You made enough in one afternoon for this?" Rowan was incredulous.

Samik shrugged. "You were right; the people here have good taste. One man called me 'The Street-Corner Sensation of Clifton.'" He swallowed and pointed. "But let's talk about you."

"What about me?"

Samik stretched out a lazy hand and poured more tea. "You need to get out there. You're always practicing or busking or running errands."

"So?" Rowan bridled. "I need to do all those things."

"Yes, yes. But you also need to meet people, find out who is looking for players and put yourself in their path. Sell your wares."

"I know lots of people here," Rowan muttered. Samik kept silent and waited. Rowan might know people, but he wasn't making contact with them. Avoiding them, more like. Samik had to be careful though—Rowan was touchy. If pushed too hard, he would just dig in his heels and close his ears.

Instead, Rowan sighed and gave up the pretense. "You're right. I know you're right. When I used to come here with my family, it was like a big holiday—if we weren't playing, we were going to hear someone else, talking music with my father's friends, running around with the other kids... My ma used to get mad at me 'cause I'd come home so late."

He looked at Samik and flopped his hand on the table helplessly. "But I'm not a kid anymore, and I don't know how to do this on my own."

He seemed wary, as if braced for ridicule. But Samik was on another mission altogether.

"So," said Samik briskly. "Tonight we go drinking. We will put you back into circulation, and I will tell you my news."

SAMIK WAS GLAD TO SEE Rowan's features relax as they strode through the dark streets, torch-lit for the festival. The rain was a mere mist on their faces, and the streets were full of revelers with no more pressing business than to enjoy a few hours with their friends. And, for once, Rowan was one of them. He actually had a little spring in his step, Samik noticed, smiling with satisfaction at the sight.

It was true that it would help Rowan's job prospects to circulate a little. But that had just been the lure. Mostly, Samik wanted to remind his new friend how to have fun.

Samik knew exactly where he was going. "The Rusty Snail, I think. You know it?" Big, crowded and noisy, it was probably not a favorite place for musicians to play. It was, however, a very good place to meet up with other people.

Rowan nodded. "How do you know so much about Clifton watering holes?"

"Watering holes. I don't know that expression. I like it." Samik grinned at Rowan. "Watering holes are not hard to learn about. You just have to go to them."

"And here I thought you were busy earning us cream pastries when you were out."

"There's a time for work and a time for play," Samik countered, quoting his granny. "Now, we should be early enough to get a seat, but you aren't allowed to stay in it all night. Two mugs, and then we launch forth and—"

Samik stopped midsentence, frozen in place, a hand held out to bar Rowan's progress. He grabbed Rowan's arm and pulled him into a dark side alley, shrinking back against the dark wall.

"What—?" Samik clapped a hand over Rowan's mouth, urging silence. He cocked his head, straining to hear. Tarzine. Men's voices speaking Tarzine.

As the voices drew closer, Rowan's eyes widened, showing Samik that he heard it too. Samik eased his hand away from Rowan's face.

Gradually, the voices grew clear—a loud, somewhat argumentative exchange among three or four men. Rowan glanced at Samik, and his face became alarmed. He reached out and pulled Samik deeper into the alley, motioning to his hair. Samik stared at him blankly for a moment, not understanding, and then his hand flew to his head. His bright hair must have caught the light from one of the fluttering torches that lit the street.

With a whispered curse, Samik eased into a crouch, far from the torch's flare. What to do? He didn't know for sure that they were Jago's men, but he couldn't risk being seen by them, just in case.

"Try to get a look at them," Samik whispered to Rowan. They didn't know him at all, would not even notice him in the busy streets.

Rowan peered around the corner of the alley, then with a deep breath straightened up and stepped smartly into the street, stopping to look as though he meant to cross. Then he melted back into the alley.

"Give it a minute," he muttered. "They're almost gone."

Samik waited impatiently, then blurted, "Well?"

"They're headed toward Provisioner's Row. I couldn't see much. They looked big. Bright clothes. One was bald—the torches shone off his head even brighter than your hair."

Bald. Samik felt the hair lift along the back of his neck. The man in his dream? He had never thought that Rowan could be in danger from Jago. "Probably traders or sailors on shore leave," he said. But he didn't really believe it, and Rowan's doubtful face showed he was not convinced. It would be unusual for sailors to wander this far from their port of call.

"Dance troupe?" Rowan suggested. Tarzine dancers were renowned for their skill and showmanship, and a troupe would do very well at the Clifton festival.

Samik shrugged. "They sound a bit rough around the edges for dancers." Then he straightened himself and slapped Rowan on the back. "But then, everyone becomes rougher around the edges after a few pots. Let's go."

Rowan held back. "Are you sure you want to—?"

"Yes, yes." Samik spread his hands as if to say, *Why not?* "They went that way, we go this way. We need not cross paths again." He gathered his hair into a ponytail and flapped it up and down. "But I will have to do something about this." Even here in Prosper, where blond hair was more common, his long pale hair stood out too much.

He was doubly glad, now, that his new plan would soon be under way. The best way to keep himself—and Rowan—safe was to move on, and soon.

FIFTEEN

At least Aydin was showing a little caution. Rowan was glad to see him take a good long look over the room—already filling up—before selecting a seat at the back table, near the scullery door. It gave them a view of most of the taproom, as well as a handy escape hatch.

They nodded to the other drinkers sharing the long trestle table and settled themselves at one end. Aydin took a sip of his dark stout, grimaced (Rowan didn't ask why—he could well imagine Aydin's views on Prosperian ale), and dove right in.

"So," he said, his pale eyes intent. "I am going into business."

Rowan didn't know what he had been expecting, but it wasn't this.

"Really?"

Aydin nodded. "With Armstrong." He smirked. "Armstrong," he repeated. "What a name."

Rowan was sure he had never heard the name before. "Who's Armstrong?"

"You know, the man who helped fix our wheel."

Or rather, the man who volunteered his servant to fix our wheel, thought Rowan.

"You mean he's hiring you?"

A firm headshake sunk that notion. "Partners."

"Partners," Rowan repeated. Armstrong, from what he had seen, was a wealthy man. Aydin had a pocketful of coins. So with nothing to invest in a business, how had Aydin talked his way into a partnership? "Doing what?"

Aydin flashed him a grin. "He wants to bring decent wine to Prosper. I know where decent wine is to be had. His money, my know-how. I take him to Tarzine wine-makers, translate, negotiate price, select the wine—with his guidance on local tastes, of course, though I must say local tastes leave a lot to be desired—and he ships them here. I get all expenses up front, and a share of the sales." Another grin. "It's brilliant."

Aydin waited expectantly while Rowan absorbed this information. Finally, he lost patience. "Perhaps the social graces are different here. In my country, one would say some-thing along the lines of 'Congratulations. How wonderful. A toast to your success.' Any one of those would be suitable."

"But—" Was Rowan missing something? He didn't think so. "How can you do that without going to the Tarzine lands?"

Aydin rolled his eyes. "Obviously, I will be going to the Tarzine lands. That is where the growers are."

"But you can't. You're supposed to stay here until it's safe."

"I will be perfectly safe." Aydin's long hand flapped carelessly. "Cut and dye my hair, arrive in these dismal Prosperian clothes with a group of Prosperian traders. We visit two or three key vineyards and are back on a ship before anyone is the wiser. Then we wait for the wine to arrive." His airy manner changed when he saw Rowan's reaction. "Oh, what? You have a better plan for me?"

Rowan hadn't even realized he was slowly shaking his head. He stopped at the Tarzine's annoyed tone.

"You think I should just hang around here and beg on street corners forever?"

"What do you mean, *beg*?" Now they were both bristling, and Aydin's dismissive wave did nothing to set things right. But his next words did.

"All I know about my brother is that he can feed himself. I don't know if he is really all right. I don't know if Jago is alive, if my family is safe. You have had a great loss, yes. I don't mean to compare. But at least you know. This is business, and I would do it regardless. But I also need to find out where things stand."

"You won't go home, will you?" Now Rowan was really alarmed, even though he understood better. Imagine if he had been away and only heard his family was sick and then…nothing. It would drive him mad. But Aydin was shaking his head.

"I am not that stupid. But I will get news from the vintners and send a letter home just before I board ship." He offered a weak smile, and Rowan had a glimpse of the loneliness and worry Aydin hid so well. "So little, yet it is still much better than nothing at all—yes?"

This time Rowan found himself nodding. "I guess it is. But Heska's teeth, be careful, Aydin." And then, belatedly, he offered his hand. "Congratulations. I guess I'd better get another round, so we can toast your success."

The front of the room had filled up while they talked, and Rowan had to wait at a counter lined three-deep with customers. He nodded at a couple of people he recognized, but they weren't close enough to actually talk to. He was just about to place his order when he caught the eye of a russet-haired girl. She didn't look familiar, but her eyebrows shot up in seeming recognition when she saw him, and then she smiled and waggled her mug at him.

Rowan smiled back vaguely, furiously trying to remember who she was. He drew a blank, lifted his fingers to signal "two" to the overworked barkeep, and only as he was paying did he realize what was going on. His cheeks did a slow burn, as much at his own slow wits as the girl's invitation. Gods, hadn't he spent all last summer wishing some girl would express the least interest in him?

He picked up the two mugs and pushed his way back through the crowd. He checked over his shoulder—she was still watching him, and her two girlfriends too. Offering an apologetic shrug, he hurried to his seat.

"I shouldn't be allowed to have this," he groaned as he planted the two mugs on the table.

"Why? Because you took so long fetching it?"

"Nope. Couldn't do anything about that." Rowan slumped onto the bench and rested his chin in his hands, defeated. "A girl invited me to join her, and I ran away." He couldn't believe he was even admitting it.

Aydin's hoot of laughter made him wish he hadn't. "Was she pretty?"

"I don't know." Rowan considered. "I guess. Yes. What does it matter? Pretty or not, she's gone."

Aydin shook his head. "I don't think so." He flicked his eyes above Rowan's shoulder.

Rowan looked around. She was heading straight for him, mug in hand. Without her girlfriends.

"Hello, lads," she said. "Mind if I sit for a bit?"

She choose a spot on the bench across from Rowan. "You're the box player."

Direct hazel eyes appraised him. So it was a business call, this. Rowan smiled, hoping it would cover the painful mix of relief and disappointment that hit him.

"I am."

"Saw you at the showcase. You're good." She held out a hand. "I'm Shay."

"Rowan. This is my friend Aydin." Shay's eyes lingered over Aydin's striking features, and for the first time it occurred to Rowan that the Tarzine's blond hair and high cheekbones might add up to good looks. The smile the two exchanged confirmed his hunch. *It would be just my luck*, thought Rowan. *Lose out to a foreigner with stork legs and bad manners.* But Shay turned back to him and got right to the point.

"I play in my uncle's band—Marten Waterford." Rowan had heard of him, though he couldn't recall having heard him play. "He's got a spot open for the pipes." She grinned. "But I'm thinking a button box would be that much better."

"I'd have to agree with you there," Rowan said. Funny how much easier it was to talk music than, well, just talk. "But what does your uncle think about it?"

"He thinks I am probably wrong," she confessed cheerfully. "But he's open-minded enough to admit he may just be clinging to what he's used to. And he says I should invite you to come play with us tomorrow afternoon so he can judge for himself."

Rowan's heart kicked into a trot that had nothing to do with flirting. This could be the chance he needed. He cut his eyes quickly to Aydin, who was studiously watching a fly labor up the side of his mug. The smirk on his face was just what Rowan had expected to see. If this worked out, Aydin would forever take credit for having flung Rowan into the path of employment.

And so he had. But it was up to Rowan now. Up to him, as well, to be careful not to jump too quickly into a situation he'd regret.

"I'd love to, of course," he replied and listened carefully while Shay told him where and when.

"Family band, is it?" he asked when she was done. He wasn't sure he wanted to be the odd man out in a family group. But Shay shook her head.

"Not really. I'm the only relative. The only young one too." She grinned. "Another reason I'm pushing for you and your box."

Rowan nodded, shy again. "Well, thanks very much for the invite. I'll see you tomorrow then."

Shay hesitated, then stood up. "Right. Nice to meet you both."

She was turning away when Aydin spoke up. "Wait!" He waited until she sat down again (looking a bit pink and breathless, Rowan thought glumly) and then asked, "Do you know anything about hair dye?"

SIXTEEN

Rowan woke up with a start. He was hot...and thirsty. And he had to pee, urgently. He flipped back the covers, swung his legs over the side of his bunk and sat up. A lightning fork of pain stabbed behind his eyeballs. Stifling a groan, he hunched against it and waited until it subsided into flickering heat lightning. Then he stood, braced against the second wave of pain that flared in protest, and stumbled through the dark caravan to the door.

It was getting light outside, very early dawn. The grass underfoot was wet with dew, the air sweet and cool. Rowan would have taken deep, grateful breaths of it if his tongue hadn't shriveled into a dry lump and glued itself against the roof of his mouth. He didn't bother with the latrines on the other side of the campsite—he just picked his way to the back of the caravan, braced himself against it and let fly.

Gods, no wonder his bladder ached. How much had he drunk last night? He couldn't remember. He couldn't remember coming home either, or how—he winced as a new pain claimed his attention—he had bruised his hipbone.

Water. Apparently all the water in his body had been sucked into his bladder. He wanted to wade into a lake and soak it up like a sponge.

Back in the caravan, Rowan dippered water out of the bucket, chugged it right from the ladle and started in on another.

Too late, he realized his mistake. His stomach lurched, then rebelled altogether. There was barely time to get back outside before he was on his knees, vomiting into the trampled grass outside the door. Each violent retch brought a new stab of pain to his head, so that when he was finally done, he just sat back on the step and rested, limp and miserable, against the caravan.

At that moment Aydin decided to investigate, throwing open the door and ramming it into Rowan's back.

"OW! Heska's teeth! Hang on, can't you?"

Rowan shifted himself off the side of the step and sat, miserable and seething, as Aydin emerged and took in the sorry scene.

"Not feeling well?"

Rowan glared. "It's not enough that you got me poisonously drunk, now you try to push me into my own puke?"

Aydin's eyebrows lifted in innocent outrage. "Surely, it's the other way round. Here I am in painful need of a piss, and you plant that mess right in front of the door so I am sure to land in it!" He stepped delicately around Rowan's vomit and disappeared behind the caravan.

LATER—MUCH LATER—that morning, Rowan gave up on his bunk and sat hunched at the table, trying to make himself function.

"What did you do to me last night?" he demanded.

Aydin, sprawled in a chair, looking pale and puffy himself, offered a brief echo of his usual lavish shrug. "I'm pretty sure I got you a job. That is, if you don't bollocks it up."

Rowan sat up, stricken. "I have to play today! Oh, crap on a stick. I'm dead before I start!"

"Not at all." Aydin levered himself upright and busied himself in the galley, suddenly brisk. "Follow Dr. Aydin's instructions, and all will be well." He turned around and pointed officiously. "You wash up and get dressed. I will make the healing potion."

Minutes later, Rowan was peering into a glass half full of slime. "What is this?"

"Special Tarzine remedy. Death to anyone who reveals the ingredients."

Rowan cast a suspicious eye at the Tarzine. "So why aren't you drinking any?"

Aydin shrugged, the full rippling roll this time. "I don't have to audition today." The grin he aimed at Rowan was pure evil. "It works, but you have to really need it."

"Why?" But one look at the ugly concoction answered his question. There was raw egg in there, that was plain, but what was that green froth?"

Aydin's laugh confirmed it. "You should maybe drink it outside…just in case."

ROWAN TRIED DESPERATELY to keep down something his entire body wanted to be rid of. He stood like a horse that had been run into the ground—head down, sides heaving, breath bellowing in violent snorts. *Think about something else*, he told himself—but he couldn't. All he could summon to mind was the way that stuff had slid down his throat.

He gagged, clapped a hand over his mouth and flared his nostrils as he sucked in air.

"Something wrong?"

Rowan goggled his eyes left and then let his hands fall in dismay.

Shay. What was she doing here? Rowan raked a hand through his jumbled curls, his nausea forgotten. Gods, he must look terrible.

She took a step closer and confirmed his fears. "You look terrible. Are you sick?"

Rowan was still too cotton-headed to make up a lie. "Drank too much last night," he admitted.

Shay's features tightened. "Do you have a problem with drinking?" she asked point-blank. "If you do, best tell me now. My uncle won't abide a drunk in his band, not after last time."

Rowan made a poor attempt at a smile. "My problem with drinking is that I can't do it. You can ask Aydin."

She narrowed her eyes at him, then gave a tiny nod. "I hope you're in better shape than this when you play with us later."

"I will be," Rowan promised, without any conviction. Though, come to think of it, he did feel a little better… maybe. His attention returned to Shay. She looked as fresh as if she'd sprung out of the dew. He still had no idea why she was here. "Um, did you want to—?"

The door banged open, and Aydin stepped out. His blond hair had resembled a haystack the last Rowan had see it. Now it hung in a brushed, gleaming sheet to his shoulders.

"Shay! I hoped that was you. Did you find what we need?" The peaky look had vanished, Rowan noticed. Aydin was all startling blue eyes and chiseled cheekbones, and Shay brightened visibly when he appeared. She pulled a bundle out from under her arm and waggled it with a grin. "Lucky for you, I found black walnut dye—much better than henna. I don't really think having bright-orange hair would make you less noticeable, do you?"

Now he remembered. Aydin had enlisted Shay to cut and dye his hair today.

Well, he would leave them to it. He'd take Wolf and go for a walk, try to blow the cobwebs out of his brain. Then a proper wash, eat a bit and warm up for his audition. His heart quickened at the thought. He really wanted this job. He might change his mind when he met Marten or heard the band, but he was determined it wouldn't be his own failings that might lose him the job.

"WHAT DO YOU THINK?"

Shay frowned at her handiwork, looking, Rowan thought, justifiably worried.

Aydin sat in a chair in front of the caravan, most of his hair piled at his feet.

The dye job had been quite successful, except for the brown stain on Aydin's temple, where it had run. His hair was now very dark brown, though with an odd, almost charcoal-gray cast to it. The haircut was another tale. Aydin's straight, fine hair showed every scissor cut, and Shay was clearly not an experienced barber. The result was a choppy patchwork that was anything but inconspicuous.

Rowan hesitated. He wanted to burst out laughing, but he didn't want to offend Shay.

"He certainly looks different."

Aydin raised an eyebrow. "But?"

This was no joking matter, Rowan reminded himself. Aydin's life might even depend on this disguise.

"The haircut's too...people will notice it too much."

Aydin scowled at Shay, who colored and said defensively, "He wanted it longer on top and short underneath, and I didn't really know how—"

"All one length," Rowan pronounced. "You want a home haircut, it has to be the same length all over. Short."

He shrugged. "Either that, or go to a barber." Shay smiled at him gratefully, and Rowan basked in this little chance to redeem himself in her eyes. He gazed at Aydin, who looked uncharacteristically vulnerable with his chunky hair and bare neck and sulky look. Rowan was trying to remember...

"My father wanted his hair really short one summer when we had a long hot spell," he said slowly. "My ma..." He walked up to Aydin and took a section of hair between his fingers. "I think she did it like this." Rowan held out his hand, and Shay handed over the scissors. "Hold it vertically, and then cut just above your fingers so they measure the length." Shay nodded encouragement, and Rowan snipped. A fringe of dark hair fluttered to the ground.

A couple of musicians from a nearby caravan strolled by. They nodded and grinned at the makeshift barbershop.

"Everyone in the camp can see you here," Rowan muttered. He handed the scissors back to Shay. "Here. Just work your way all around his head—I'll clean up these long cuttings. Then he'll just be a guy getting a trim."

He was dropping the last clump of hair into the garbage pail when two bells sounded. The gatekeepers at the players' camp sounded the bells every hour from midmorning to midnight to help everyone meet their various engagements.

Shay gave a yelp of alarm. "Blast! I have to go. It won't look good if I'm late 'cause of you."

I didn't make you late, Rowan wanted to protest, but Shay was running on. "You can finish up here, right? And be at Traveler's Rest at three bells. Don't be late!"

"Traveler's Rest. I wonder how long it took them to think up such an original name?" Aydin smirked. There seemed no end to his amusement at Prosperian names. Unimaginative or not, it was one of Rowan's favorite venues—a musician's room, with good acoustics and a nice spacious alcove for the band.

Brandishing the scissors, he advanced on Aydin. "Looks like you're stuck with me. But believe me, I can't possibly make it worse."

"How do I look—honestly?" asked Aydin.

"Like a half-plucked chicken," said Rowan solemnly, pressing his lips tight to keep from grinning.

Aydin clucked—twice—and then they both were cackling with laughter.

SEVENTEEN

Traveler's Rest was already busy, and the band in full swing when Rowan arrived. He had come early, hoping he could lurk in the back unnoticed and listen for a while.

He could tell right away they were good. That crossed one worry off his list: what to do if he were offered a place with poor players. "If I accept, I might lose a place with a better band," he had fretted to Aydin. He would have liked to ask Timber's advice, but there was no time to search out the older man.

"And if you decline, you might end up with nothing." Aydin had no trouble finishing the thought, which was obvious enough. That didn't make it easier to work out though.

He threaded his way through the drinkers to get a look at his potential colleagues. Shay's red hair shone in the dim room. She played with assurance and grace, not as well as

Rowan's father, but not needing any allowances for her age either. Rowan looked next for her uncle.

Marten Waterford gave an impression of squareness: a broad face topped by a full head of wiry, graying hair, wide shoulders, big hands. It made a comical contrast to his instrument—the wood flute looked too dainty for him, as though he'd be more likely to snap it in half than make music with it. That had been Rowan's mother's instrument, and he had a sudden, vivid memory of how she had looked playing, her body swaying a little to the rhythm and her lips pursed just so as she blew across the mouth hole.

He hadn't time for more than a hurried glance at the other two players—on tenor mandola and, Rowan was delighted to see, a drum—when Shay caught his eye and waved him over. He was on.

"We'll play first and talk later, yes? Just play along on whatever you know, and we'll give you some requests in a bit." Marten had a deep voice to match his solid build, and the slightly brusque manner of a man used to being in charge. But the crinkled lines around his eyes suggested good humor as well, Rowan thought. He hoped so, anyway. He took the seat offered him by the mandola player and flipped the latches on his case.

It was hard work, playing with new people, without the comfortable patterns and easy communication developed over the years with his family. Though Rowan knew most of the tunes, he was feeling his way through them, trying to find the openings where the piper used to play and adapt to the variations any long-standing group of players brought to their music. When they finally took a break and Marten shooed the others away from their table so they could talk privately, Rowan was not at all sure how well he had done.

"Your parents were fine players," Marten began. "A great loss."

Rowan nodded. Sheer frequency had made it easier to handle condolences, and Marten's were blessedly brief. What bothered him now was how rarely his sister was mentioned. *Ettie was a great loss too*, he wanted to yell—but you couldn't blame people for focusing on the ones they knew.

"And you do them credit, Rowan, without a doubt." Rowan braced himself for a *but* to follow.

"I have to admit, I was reluctant to give up the pipes. They're an old and honored tradition, you know, and have been part of our sound since I began. But"—and here Marten spread out his big hands with a self-deprecating laugh—"you play the shite out of that thing, and the crowd loves it. So if you're interested, let's talk business."

Relief washed over Rowan and left him almost giddy. He really wanted this job, had known that almost as soon as he started playing. Marten seemed like a leader to trust, the players were tight and capable, and he had always wanted to add a drummer to his family's ensemble, loving the drama and drive a simple goatskin could add. Best of all, there was another player his age in the group—a player he was already on his way to being friends with. He'd never find a better fit.

"Yes, sir," he managed. "I'm definitely interested."

Now Marten's grin was wide and open. "Right. Then let's get a couple of pints, and I'll fill you in."

Arrangements were easily made: Rowan would start playing with them in Clifton right away, but then he was free to make the journey to his uncle's and rejoin them at the start of the summer season. Like most players, Marten's group traveled a good deal through the summer, but they stayed in the royal seat of Kingstown for the winter. "The king has his royal musicians, of course, but there is plenty more work," Marten assured Rowan. "The nobles in the city rarely hire a band for the season like the country gentry do—they prefer to vary their entertainment, depending on the occasion. But there are so many occasions that, between that and the local watering holes, we never go hungry.

"I have a house there," he added, answering Rowan's next question. "You are welcome to Ash's old room."

"It sounds great," said Rowan. "I'd be honored."

IT WOULD BE VERY DIFFERENT, living in the biggest city in Prosper instead of the small world of a country estate. Less secure, certainly, but Rowan couldn't help being excited at the prospect. He tried to imagine it as he walked back to the caravan: the crowded streets, the lavish affairs thrown by the king's entourage, and the rich merchants, the rough taverns and lodgings clustered around the dockyards. What kind of house did Marten own, and who else would be living there?

Marten had said he would pay half the cost to winter the mules and store the caravan if Rowan kept it, explaining they were already too cramped in his smaller rig. It would be expensive in the city though. Rowan wondered if he might leave his rig with his Uncle Ward instead.

Lost in his thoughts, Rowan didn't realize at first that the guard at the gate was talking to him.

"Sorry?"

"I asked if that friend of yours is in some kind of trouble."

"Why?" The question came out too sharp, Rowan's alarm plain for the guard to see.

"I thought as much." The man, a plump old fellow who had worked the gate to the musician's park for years and seemed hardly to notice who came and went, nodded in satisfaction. "Bit of an odd one, your friend, even among this lot." He cast his eyes over the park, as if cataloguing in his mind the many oddities of musicians.

Rowan wanted to shake the old bugger. "What happened?"

The guard's eyes fixed on him, bright with curiosity. "A bunch of foreigners came asking after him. Big men, and rough, looking for a tall young 'un with long blond hair and a fiddle."

Rowan's heart sank. Jago's men had found Aydin. He looked wildly toward his caravan, torn between racing over to see if Aydin was there and trying to find out more. The guard's hand came down on his arm, staying him.

"Never fear, young sir, they learned nothing from me. I saw you mucking with his hair this morning. I said I hadn't seen no one like that. They tried to push through and look around, but I told them anyone comes in the park unauthorized, I sound the alarm."

Rowan glanced at the man, aware of the courage it would take to stand up to thugs like that. His pink, round face was indignant. "I don't take kindly to bully boys, and that's a fact. Thinking they could swagger in here like they owned the place!" He shrugged. "Anyway, your friend wasn't here. He ain't back yet neither."

NOT KNOWING WHERE TO LOOK for Aydin, Rowan decided to stay put at the caravan. He tried to work on some of the tunes he'd be playing with Marten's band tomorrow, but it was useless—his mind kept hopping like a flea back to Aydin. Where was he? What if Jago's men had already found him? What if they came back to the players' camp to try the night guard? This time they might not take *no* for an answer...

It was well dark when Aydin finally burst in the door, breathing hard. Wolf trotted in after him.

"They're asking around the pubs for me," he gasped.

"Here too," said Rowan. "The guard sent them packing, but..." He shook his head. They both knew that had only bought a bit of time.

Aydin was back by his bunk, hauling out clothes and stuffing them into his pack.

"Time for me to go," he said.

"What, now?" A stupid question, since the caravan was clearly no longer safe, but the sight of Aydin's hurried, careless packing only ratcheted up Rowan's anxiety. "But where will you go?"

Aydin stopped then and turned to face him. "To Armstrong's. I'll be safe there. He lives way on the outskirts of town, and Jago's men are looking for an itinerant viol player in the thick of the festival." Aydin looked around the narrow room, decided he was done and cinched his pack up tight. "Anyway, we'll be gone soon." He flashed a quick grin, regaining his old bravado. "They'll be tramping around Prosper, and I'll be part of a rich merchant's retinue, touring the vineyards of my homeland."

"I'll walk you to Armstrong's," Rowan blurted out. "See you safe arrived."

Aydin began to protest and then stopped midsentence. His hands dropped to his sides, the bluster gone.

"Thank you," he said simply. "For this, and for everything."

They left the park cautiously and walked the long way around, avoiding the center of town. Wolf paced beside them, leashed for once. They made a few false turns, and it was nearing midnight when they entered the quiet, wealthy neighborhood where Armstrong lived. Aydin stopped at the end of a long street.

"We'll say goodbye here, I think," he said. "Better for you if you don't know exactly where I am."

"You're sure you'll be able to rouse him?" asked Rowan.

"Yes, yes. Always the mother! If not, I will sleep on his back porch and rouse him in the morning."

There was an awkward silence, and then Aydin spoke in a rush: "Will you take Wolf? He likes you, and he hates sea travel. And I will be less noticeable without him."

"Yes," said Rowan, strangely touched. "Of course. If you're sure."

Aydin reached out to put the leash into Rowan's hand. "Then I think that's all." He looked up, just past Rowan's head, and with a formal little bow said, "Goodbye, lovely Ettie. Be at peace."

Ettie. Rowan had been forgetting her, hadn't thought of her for days. There'd been no voices or breaths on his neck to remind him either, not since the day he'd ignored her and broken the wheel. Guilt washed over him along with a strange thought: he wouldn't even have known about her, if not for Aydin. But Aydin had already turned back to him.

"Goodbye, Rowan Redwing, button box player. It has been an honor." And then, taking Rowan completely by surprise, the young Tarzine stepped forward, hugged him and kissed him on the mouth—hard. Then he turned and strode, with his long, storklike pace, into the dark.

Rowan was so taken aback that he just stood there, but when Wolf whined and pulled at the leash, Rowan had to coax the great dog to let his master go and make the long trek home with him.

It was all very confusing. Rowan had thought he'd be happy to see the end of his odd, irritating guest—but he wasn't.

He should have been annoyed at being stuck with Wolf's care—the dog ate more than he did, for starters—but in truth he was glad of Wolf's company. And that kiss. It was probably just how Tarzines said goodbye; another flamboyant gesture, like their dress and their music. But he couldn't quite convince himself, and his mind kept returning to it as he walked through the quiet night. He'd been jealous of Shay's obvious attraction to Aydin. What if all along Aydin had been more interested in *him*?

Well, he'd never know. *Chalk it up to the mystery that is Aydin*, he told himself. *May the gods keep him safe.*

EIGHTEEN

The festival was winding up, and Rowan was too busy playing and making plans with the Waterford group and preparing for his overdue visit to Ward and Cardinal's house to miss Aydin much. He did keep an anxious ear open for news of the men on Aydin's trail and was relieved to find that after another day or two of combing the pubs and busking corners, they had apparently given up.

Rowan planned to travel with the others along the Coast Road past Stormy Head. From there they would continue on to Kingstown, Prosper's royal city. *Aydin would have played that one to the limit*, he thought ruefully, remembering his friend's endless amusement at perfectly ordinary names.

Rowan's route would then take him north from the Coast Road, deep into sheep country. He wasn't really looking forward to another dull journey along pokey country roads, or even to the reunion at the end. He had managed to grow a skin over his grief, but for his aunt and uncle it would be fresh and raw. And they would not understand, he knew, why he had not come to them immediately after his family's death. He hardly understood it himself. When he looked back on those days, it seemed like he had existed in a thick fog that didn't let him think beyond the next town.

SHAY RODE BESIDE HIM for most of the journey. "I hate riding inside the cart," she said. "Makes me pukey. And Marten doesn't leave much room on the seat when he's driving."

Wolf, who had claimed the front seat for himself, seemed a bit put out at being displaced. He climbed into the back of the caravan and flopped on the floor. "I guess he misses Aydin," said Rowan. "Normally, he'd be loping along with his nose to the road."

"You must miss him too," offered Shay.

Rowan shrugged. "I guess. He's..." He hesitated, not sure there was a word for what Aydin was.

"Really handsome," Shay finished. She cocked her head, her gaze dreamy, as if to summon up every good-looking detail.

"So I gather," said Rowan shortly, remembering the effortless way Aydin talked girls into giving him food, sneaking him into cellars, cutting his hair. He wished he had half that ease and charm, instead of being awkward and average-looking.

"Ah, now, I'm sorry." Shay laid her hand on his arm, just briefly. "I didn't mean to make your eye start up again. You're perfectly fine-looking yourself."

"My eye?"

"You know, that little twitch. You hardly do it at all anymore."

Rowan stared at her blankly, and then his cheeks burned hot with humiliation as he felt the fleeting pull at the right side of his face. He *had* felt that before, lots of time, without even noticing.

"Oh, shite. You didn't know. Heska's teeth, I'm sorry." Now Shay was red-cheeked and embarrassed.

Rowan stared at the road, his jaw set. "Do I do it a lot?"

"No. Aydin said you did it a lot when he first met you. And I saw it a few times that night I first talked to you. But never when you're playing, and like I said, hardly at all lately."

Rowan nodded, trying not to show the relief he felt. "Must be from when I was sick," he said, still not meeting her eye.

"Yes. Anyway, it's nothing. I was stupid to even mention it." Shay glanced at him, trying out a tentative smile. "Maybe we should not talk for a bit, so I don't make any more blunders."

Rowan smiled back in spite of himself. "It's much harder to be annoyed with you than with Aydin. He never hesitates to blunder on."

SAMIK RESTED HIS HEAD against the cushioned leather seat of Armstrong's carriage. This, he reflected, was the proper way to travel, not having your teeth jolted out of your head in a plodding cart. And the inn they had stayed in last night at Stormy Head had been first class. The food, the lodgings, the work itself—everything was better with Armstrong. Still, it had been hard to leave Rowan, and harder still to give up K'waaf.

Maybe he should have told Rowan about his dream, warned him to be careful. That dream had stayed with him all these weeks, and the sighting of the bald-headed Tarzine had been chilling confirmation. But Rowan didn't believe in true dreams or premonitions, and even if he did, what could he do? No, it was better this way. Once it was clear that Samik and Rowan had parted ways, Jago's thugs would lose interest in Rowan. And if the danger happened to be from some other bald man, some petty criminal, K'waaf's presence alone was enough to deter most small-time thieves. If not, he would defend Rowan fiercely.

With a sigh, he shook off these thoughts and turned his attention to the road ahead. It had taken longer than he had expected for Armstrong to make his preparations, and he had been on edge every extra day he spent in Clifton. It was good to feel safe again.

"Second thoughts, my young friend?" Armstrong had been watching the road go by, but turned at Samik's long sigh.

"Not at all." Samik grinned. "I was just thinking how long it's been since I've had a really good wine."

"Not much longer now." Armstrong returned the smile. "Then we'll toast to a great venture. You and I are going to make a good deal of coin together."

Samik nodded. "Will we reach Kingstown today, do you think?" Stormy Head was a smallish harbor, mostly fishing boats. Kingstown, the country's largest trade center, was where they would find a ship to take them to Guara.

Armstrong shook his head. "Not unless you want to travel into the wee hours of morning, and I don't. There are a couple of guest houses along the way that are not too grim." He grimaced. "I'm still embarrassed that I didn't even know we had to sail north, not south."

The first ship's captain Armstrong approached would have set him straight, but Samik didn't tell him so. He liked the fact that he had already proved his worth on this trip, and didn't mind if that worth was exaggerated in his new partner's mind.

"So where do we land, somewhere around here?" Armstrong had asked as they hunched over a map of the island, planning their trip. He pointed to the little harbor of Rath Turga. "Or maybe this place, Baskir. It looks bigger."

"No, no!" Samik had been more amused than alarmed. "You see these"—he peered at the map to read the Prosperian name—"yes, of course, these Talons," he said. "Very treacherous to sail past. Tides, shoals, fog, shifting winds—no sailor wants to thread between the Talons and these islands, so you'd have to head way out to sea to miss them altogether. And then," he continued, "you head back into the badlands."

"The badlands?" It was clear Armstrong knew next to nothing of the Tarzine lands.

"The southern part of the country is essentially lawless," Samik explained, sweeping his hand from Baskir south. "You could be taken by pirates before you ever landed."

Only when he saw the alarm in Armstrong's face did Samik realize he shouldn't have been so cavalier about the dangers. Rampaging warlords were not something Prosperians took for granted. They didn't realize that only the Tarzine pirates' superstitious dread of the "Talons" kept them safe; a potent mix of legend and actual shipwrecks made even sailing past them taboo. Samik wondered how long it would be until some enterprising warlord overcame his crew's reluctance and braved the sea god's curse.

"You don't need to worry," he rushed to assure his partner. "We go this way—north, a smooth sail into Guara. It's a well-established trade route, perfectly safe. The vineyards are mainly in this area, spreading inland from Maug Nazir. That's the stronghold of the empire."

THE CARRIAGE SLOWED, then came to a gentle halt. Not their guest house already? Samik cranked up the little blind that kept out the wind and dust to peek out. No, they were in thick woodland. Maybe a problem with the road or the horse, he thought, remembering the breakneck descent with Rowan that had broken their wheel.

He was just about to ask Armstrong if he should jump out and check when he felt something digging into his back. It hurt, and when he arched his back to relieve the pressure it followed him. He was twisting around to see what it was when Armstrong's voice stopped him.

"Just stay where you are, if you please, and hands nice and high against the carriage wall. No, I wouldn't wiggle around—that's my short sword you're feeling. Wouldn't want a nasty accident."

Samik froze. But even though his body obeyed, at first his mind couldn't make sense of the words. Was it a joke? They had discussed Armstrong's sword before the journey. Samik had been glad to see him strap it on. "You can't be too careful on the roads," the older man had commented. They had planned to buy one for Samik before boarding ship.

"Armstrong, what is this?" he protested.

"Out of the carriage first, young sir. Nice and slow." When he did not respond, the sword dug deeper in prodding bites. Samik felt his heart ratchet up as he began to realize that whatever was going on, it was no lighthearted prank. He opened the carriage door, wondering if he could possibly pull the knife in his boot on the way out.

"Slow now, hands up high," Armstrong cautioned. They made their way out onto the road, the sword tip never losing contact with Samik's kidney. The carriage was pulled neatly to the side, Armstrong's driver Purdy still sitting with reins in hand. He didn't look at Samik, but rather ahead to...

Now he understood. Fear surged through him as he stared at the three men who waited on the road. Unlike him, they hadn't bothered to disguise their country of origin. Armstrong had betrayed him.

"Why?" he demanded. He whirled to face Armstrong, not caring that the sword tore through his coat as he turned. Perhaps, even now, he might talk him out of it, dive back into the carriage and evade his hunters. "We're partners! You said it yourself, we're going to make a lot of money. You can't just..." Samik's voice died away. The bracing gust of anger that had carried him for moment receded as if washed down a drain, along with his last hope.

Armstrong had groped into his pocket with his free hand and was now holding up an obviously weighty purse.

"Don't take it personal, my boy. It's just business. It wasn't a bad idea you had, but you know—" He twisted his wrist, so that the purse swayed to and fro before Samik's eyes. "You can't argue with cash in hand."

Heavy hands took hold of Samik, and there was no use in struggling. Three heavily muscled and armed thugs against one scrawny wine merchant? Completely pointless.

He was tied, tossed in a wagon and back on the road before it occurred to him: Armstrong hadn't taken his knife.

It didn't make his odds any better. Bound and surrounded, what could he do with a little throwing knife? But somehow, the thought of that hidden knife gave him courage.

NINETEEN

Here I am again, thought Rowan, *alone with my mules on an overgrown country road*. There'd been a bit of traffic in the first few miles of the narrow road that led to the little town where his uncle lived, but it soon dwindled away altogether. Soon, he knew, the road would rise out of the woodland and take him through open, rolling hills dotted with sheep. Rowan wondered why his uncle—or rather, Ward's father, who had started the business—hadn't set up in a busier trade center. *I guess you can either be close to the sheep or close to the market*, he thought. *And cheaper to set up out here, I bet.*

Ugh, was he really thinking about Ward's weaving business? He didn't remember feeling this lonely and bored back in the early days—before he met Aydin, and then Shay. Truth to tell, he hadn't felt much of anything back then. Now he'd grown used to company. To friends.

He was even looking forward to seeing Ward and Cardinal, now that he was on his way. But he wouldn't stay long. His band was waiting for him, and so was Shay. At least he hoped she was. Rowan liked her a lot—and was well on his way to more than liking her. He hadn't even thought red hair was pretty until he saw hers. Be careful, he told himself, and it was his father's voice he imagined. You have to work together, whether she feels the same or not.

He wasn't craving company at night though. Two nights with a guest in his caravan—not Shay, sadly, but Walker, the drummer—had seen to that. Rowan had volunteered the space on learning that the men in the band were taking turns on the floor in Marten's caravan. "Marten has partitioned off one space for me with a curtain, so I'm fine," Shay had told him. "But the others are really crowded."

So Walker had joined him, and it hadn't taken long to discover why the others had chosen him for the honor. The man snored like a ripsaw all night long, an astonishingly loud, buzzing drone punctuated by snorts, coughs and great sucking gasps that sounded like he was choking. The next morning, Shay's eyes had twinkled with mischief as she asked Rowan how he slept, and he had smiled right back and replied "Fine. You?" But he was pretty sure his bleary face betrayed his bluff.

Not this way.

"Demon's breath!" Rowan hauled on the reins, almost angry at his own spooked reaction. Had he really heard that? He peered down the shadowed arch of the road. He couldn't see much—not far ahead, a sharp bend to the right cut off his view.

"Ettie?" He spoke out loud, not caring how it sounded. "Ettie, if that's you, please tell me again so I'm sure."

He waited, hearing the creak and stamp as the mules shifted their weight, the far-off shriek of a jay, the rustle of the wind through the high branches. Slowly, the prickly feeling at the back of his neck subsided.

Turn back.

Rowan sighed. He didn't dare ignore her, not after last time. But what was he supposed to do? There was only one road to Ward and Cardinal's that he knew, and this was it.

"All right, Ettie, not this way," he agreed. "But why? Can you tell me why?"

The answer came fast but weak, like the softest whispered breath.

Samik.

IT BECAME SUFFOCATINGLY HOT in the wagon. Samik was hidden under a thick layer of horse blankets topped with an oilcloth tarp, which trapped the heat and kept out any breath of air. The thin layer of straw beneath him poked and scratched maddeningly without doing anything to soften the jolts and lurches of the wagon. He could feel bruises blooming on his shoulder, hip and cheekbone, and counted himself lucky to have no broken bones.

And yet he did not want this dark, sweltering, bone-jarring journey to end, for what came next would certainly be worse. A warlord's revenge was always terrible.

Don't think about it. But he couldn't stop himself. Fear clutched his bowels, and the struggle not to add to the misery of the wagon by fouling himself was a welcome distraction. *Wait and do it on them.* Brave words that he would never, he knew, dare to carry out.

He would never see his family or his home again. Another thing not to think about—but then again, sad was better than terrified. He pictured Merik, sitting up in bed eating soup, and hoped that by now he was demanding seconds at the dinner table. He prayed his family remained safe from Jago's rage. And then it was Rowan in his head—Rowan with his burdened air and gruff kindness, Rowan who became as free and light as the bird his family was named for when he had a button box on his knee. That kiss had probably shocked him out of his straight-laced boots. *If he only knew,* thought Samik, *how often I've wanted to do that.* No harm in stealing a quick one at their last goodbye.

A sharp turn threw Samik against the sidewall of the wagon, and he felt the ground beneath them change to something soft and resistant. *Wherever we're going, we're almost there,* he thought, and the fear flooded back in a paralyzing wave.

TURNING AROUND IS NOT SUCH a simple matter on a narrow road with a big caravan. Rowan had to get down and walk the mules backward a good five hundred paces to the little logging track he'd noticed on the way in. It was tiny and deeply rutted, and he was afraid they'd get stuck, but the mules somehow managed to back the caravan in. The tight, tricky turn back onto the road was no easy feat either, but at last he climbed back onto the seat and took up the reins.

Then he just sat there uncertainly. Alarm, confusion, even embarrassment (how would he ever explain this to Ward and Cardinal?) all roiled around inside him, making it hard to think what to do next.

GO!

It was sharp and clear, as urgent as the night he woke up in the fire, and it startled Rowan into action. He snapped the reins, shouted to the mules and urged them into a trot. He didn't know where he was going; he had to trust that Ettie would guide him. He only hoped that when he found Aydin—Samik, he corrected himself, his real name was Samik—he would know what to do.

AS SOON AS THE BLANKETS were pulled off him, Samik knew they were on the coast. That ocean smell on the wind, the sound of the surf—there was no mistaking it. But it took a minute before the sun stopped stabbing into his eyes and he could actually see.

He barely noticed the stony beach, the small, sheltered cove, the sheen of late afternoon light on the water. It was the ship that filled his vision. Even resting at anchor with its ocher sails neatly furled, the racy lines proclaimed it a Tarzine ship.

Dread and longing. He wanted to be on a ship just like that, heading home. Joking with the crew in his own language, eating and drinking something that was actually good, his parents waiting to meet them at the docks. His mother and Aunt Kir crying at the sight of him.

But this ship—this ship meant his happy vision would never come true. This ship meant death.

TWENTY

It was hours past dark, the woods on either side a black wall and the road an indistinct gray ribbon unfurling ahead of him, and still Ettie urged Rowan on. He was really listening to her now, and the harder he listened, the clearer she became. It was as if she perched, invisible and weightless, on his shoulder, guiding his path. Sometimes it seemed like her words were forming in his head, and often it seemed he could feel what she felt—her urgency, her determination.

Her alarm was contagious, and he was sure now that Samik was in real trouble. He had pushed the mules to trot for much of the way, with only short breaks at their usual ambling walk. But they were tired now and needed watering, and despite Ettie's protests, Rowan eased them to a halt.

"They need a rest, Ettie," Rowan said, no longer feeling strange about talking to the air. "They aren't used to this pace, and we need them to hold out the whole way." He didn't know how long "the whole way" was—they must be nearly back to the King's Highway. He went into the caravan and emptied both water jugs into the bucket. He might regret that, he supposed. He remembered a little creek that ran near the road somewhere along here, but in the dark it would be hard to find and treacherous to get to. No time for that.

The mules drank eagerly, but Rowan held back about half the water. He had a vague memory of his father saying it wasn't good for them to eat or drink too much before exercise, and didn't want to take the chance of giving them bloat or whatever it was. He gave them a small portion of hay each, a handful of oats, and another little drink to wash it down.

He was tired himself, his butt sore from the hard wooden seat, his back stiff from long hours on the road. He tried to walk it off while the mules munched at their feed. He felt Ettie's impatience growing by the minute.

Soon they were back on the deserted road. Even with Ettie's guidance, Rowan didn't dare trot the mules in the dark—and in any case he was pretty sure they were all trotted out. Still, they seemed ready to keep up their steady, dogged walk forever. Unable to see much of anything, Rowan put his faith in the mules' sure-footedness and turned his worried mind back to Samik.

What had happened to his friend? While it was theoretically possible that he was sick or injured or robbed and left stranded on the side of the road, Rowan didn't believe for one moment in any of these scenarios. For Samik, there was only one kind of trouble.

Rowan didn't know how much farther he had to go. He was terribly afraid he wouldn't get there—wherever "there" was—in time. He should be flying along on a galloping stallion, not plodding through mile after mile in a caravan. And once there, what could he possibly do against the likes of the Tarzine thugs they had seen in Clifton? Wolf would help, but…

Where *was* Wolf? Rowan couldn't recall seeing him for a long time…maybe since before he turned the caravan around.

"Wolf! Here, Wolf!" Nothing. The knot in his stomach clenched.

He's just gone to bed, Rowan told himself. Wolf generally did flop onto the caravan floor at first dark. Pulling the mules to a halt and tying the reins through the knothole in the buckboard, he turned and shoved his head through the canvas flap.

"Wolf? You here, boy?" Wolf at his laziest might not have come running, but he would at least thump his tail mightily on the floor. He wasn't there.

Sick with regret, Rowan tried to work out how it had happened: Wolf must have run ahead through the woods and not realized Rowan had turned around. How far behind would he be, and would he try to follow? Somehow the thought of facing whatever was to come without Wolf made the fear he'd been holding at bay scrabble in his guts. If he couldn't even look after a dog...

Gods, what a mess. The foreboding that came over Rowan then was so strong that he just wanted to hide his head in his hands and cry like a baby, to give up before he got them all killed.

Samik needs you. Ettie's voice was gentle but firm. She was right, of course. There was no time for blubbering, nothing to do but press on.

THE TARZINE MEN HAD STOPPED at a scrubby strip of open land bordering the stony beach. Not one of them spoke or even really looked at Samik. Instead, they unloaded him briskly, as if he were an awkward sort of cargo, propped him up against the side of the little cart, threaded a rope through the gaps in the boards and lashed him to it by the waist. Then they left the cart, the overburdened donkey who pulled it, and their horses, and made their way on foot down to the water. The little donkey set right in chewing at the tangled mass of pea vetch at his feet.

Samik watched them bleakly. Yelling after them, demanding or begging to be released might earn him another bruise but would accomplish precisely nothing. These men answered to one person only.

His captors, he saw, were making for a huge stack of wood piled about ten feet from the high-tide line. They took a few pieces and laid a small fire, and one hunkered over it. Soon the flames licked up. One man—tall and black-haired, with high cheekbones, dark almond-shaped eyes and catlike grace—loped back up the slope. Samik tensed when the man pulled out a curved knife, but he only set to cutting an armful of random branches and returned to the fire.

Black smoke billowed in waves as the flames were half smothered by greenery.

A signal. The fear that had been whispering and slithering and gnawing through his body for hours suddenly burst free and swallowed him whole. The strength drained out of his legs so that he sagged against the rope that cut into his stomach, and he gasped for air as an invisible icy hand squeezed at his lungs and throat. In a hot, liquid gush, his bladder and bowels let go, and he was too afraid to feel shame or disgust.

Jago was on that ship. Samik knew it, and he knew what all that wood was for too. He had the true Sight, and he had never wished more that he didn't.

"GODS' BALLS, WHAT A STINK!" The first of the three to return to the cart was an oxlike, heavily muscled man with a bald and elaborately tattooed head. He cackled with mocking laughter at the others. "Our young rooster shat himself like a baby, just standing here waiting! We'll have to watch he don't die of fright before the show starts."

Samik glared at him. He felt stronger, as if some of his fear had been cast out with his shit. The terror would be back, he knew. But for now he would give them as little satisfaction as he could.

The catlike one wrinkled his nose against the smell, making his gold nose ring flash in the late afternoon sun. He gestured impatiently. "Will we stand around inhaling it then? Go on, Voka, take him down to the strand and sluice him out."

There was grumbling and a few dark looks, but eventually Voka and the third man, the one called Tyhr, grabbed hold of Samik under each arm and hauled him down to the water. With his ankles still tied with the befouled rope, Samik was all but helpless—but he still managed to stumble against Voka and smear a little poop on his boot and pant leg. A childish revenge, but it buoyed him all the same. The thug's roar of disgust was worth the violent shove that all but dislocated Samik's shoulder.

He was returned to the wagon, dripping wet from the waist down and still fragrant, but much improved. Then he was tied up again and ignored. The sun dropped into the sea and the stars winked into sight; Jago's henchmen rummaged in their saddlebags and ate around the little fire on the beach. Samik began to hurt everywhere. Tied as he was, he couldn't change his position, scratch, or wipe the sweat off his face. His legs ached from standing, but he couldn't sit down.

Eventually, two figures lay down by the fire, and the big bald one, Voka, returned to him. He seemed to have been appointed Samik's personal keeper. "Wake me up, I'll make you sorry," he grunted as he rolled in a blanket in the wagon. "And if you crap yourself again, you'll eat it!"

"You're going to leave me standing like this all night?" The black hours yawned ahead of him.

"You want to interrupt Jago's evening? He'll come soon enough, believe me." Voka sniggered in the dark. "Enjoy your nice rest, young buck. It'll look good by comparison."

THE MOON HAD RISEN AND SET, leaving the night road darker than ever. Ettie had nudged Rowan onto the highway heading back toward Stormy Head, and then onto a side road angling toward the sea. He was grateful for the clear sky. Starlight didn't actually help him see much, but it made the darkness seem less oppressive.

Despite his anxiety, Rowan was having a hard time staying awake. The rhythm of the mules' hooves was hypnotic, and hour after hour on the hard seat seemed to numb his brain as well as his butt. More than once he felt his head jerk and his eyelids fly open, with no memory of them closing.

Stop.

Rowan snapped to attention, yanking hard on the reins and looking around wildly, as if Tarzine raiders might be advancing upon him from every direction. But the night was peaceful. He guided the mules to the side of the road, pulled the brake on the caravan and got down.

The woodland had given way to scrubby brush and open sky, giving him a view of a limitless expanse of stars and below them a vast, murmuring darkness that could only be the ocean. Ettie gave him a little push, but he hesitated. "Wait a moment," he whispered and climbed into the caravan. Groping for lamp and tinder, he made his way by lamplight to the galley and pulled open a drawer. His hands went first to his mother's biggest kitchen knife, but then settled on the slim fish-filleting blade. It was smaller, but very sharp, and it had a case that could fasten on to his belt. He could picture all too well what might happen with the other if he stumbled and fell in the dark.

Something else was nagging at him. He didn't know what he was going to find or how he was going to help, but he had no illusions of killing a bunch of Tarzine men with a fish knife. The best he could picture was that he and Samik would be running away, and while a caravan was not exactly a speedy getaway choice, it was all he had. And the mules were facing the wrong way for an escape.

He paced across the road and found it had become little more than a sandy, narrow track. There was no telling, in the dark, whether it opened up into a space where he could turn around, or dwindled into nothing. And he could have passed a handful of side roads on the way without seeing them—or none.

Ettie was prodding at him, unhappy at the delay. There was nothing he could do about the caravan. With a deep breath, Rowan left the mules behind and set off on foot down a path he could barely see.

TWENTY-ONE

After a noisy fall that left his heart hammering in alarm, Rowan dropped to his hands and knees. He followed Ettie's lead blindly, feeling his way as quietly as he could and ignoring his scraped palms.

It wasn't long before he sensed the underbrush thinning, and soon he emerged at the top of a long, bare slope to the sea. He heard the ocean clearly now and saw the glimmer of starlight on the crests of the waves. The salt breeze on his face was like a splash of cool water, bringing him fully alert. He hunkered down on his stomach and strained all his senses as he swept his eyes over the scene.

The first thing he noticed was the red glow down on the beach—the remains of a fire. He was focused on those embers, trying to see if there was any movement around them, when a soft thud practically at his elbow made him jump.

He dropped his head (as if anyone could see it, he mocked himself, but he could not override the instinct) and lay still. His stupid heart was drumming again, trying to drown out the sounds he needed to hear. So was his breath, hitching in and out in harsh noisy gasps.

Rowan closed his eyes and listened for all he was worth. Nothing. His breath calmed down.

Thud.

He'd heard that sound before, he was sure. It came again, then a creak. Then the breeze shifted a little and he smelled it—horse. There was a horse, at least one horse, tethered nearby. Maybe saddled—the tack would creak as the animal shifted its weight.

Now he raised his head and peered toward the sound. Gods, there they were, maybe twenty paces away. Two big black shapes, obvious when you knew what you were looking for. And a third, a solid rectangle. A cart or wagon of some kind.

A crunchy rustle came from the same area. Rowan had heard that before too: a body shifting on straw. There was a grunt and several loud sighing breaths as the sleeper resettled himself. At least one man then. It wasn't Samik, at least Rowan didn't think so. The voice sounded too deep.

Was Samik there? He had to be—otherwise why would Ettie have led him here? But how could he find him, or help him, if he couldn't see?

He had to try. The darkness was a hindrance, but it was also their best—maybe their only—chance of escape.

If he could find and free Samik while his guards slept, they might be able to sneak back into the bush before the alarm was raised. Ettie had shown him the way in; she would lead them out too.

"Ettie, what should I do?" Rowan breathed the words out in a fervent whisper, but there was no reply. He looked out over the ocean as if the answer lay in its ceaseless waves. A silvery rim edged the horizon—the first hint of morning to come. He had no plan, yet he had to act now.

The first thing was to find Samik. It seemed a good possibility that he was actually in the wagon or cart. He would try to circle around and come out behind the wagon. Then he would look for his friend.

SAMIK HAD NEVER DREAMED mere standing could be so painful. However he tried to shift his weight, his legs ached with a vicious insistent throb. The rope around his waist bit into his guts when he sagged with fatigue. And he was cold, the damp night breeze off the ocean sinking deep into his bones so that he could not stop shivering. The only mercy was that his captors had bound his wrists in front rather than behind him, so he was able to lean against the side of the cart and relieve some of the load on his legs that way. The thick ropes chafed his skin, but at least he wasn't crushing his own hands.

The night crept on like an endless nightmare. At one point Samik found himself crying in breathy sobs, helpless to hold it back, yet somehow able to heed Voka's warning and make next to no sound. He cried from the pain and the crushing exhaustion, but even more from the terrifying knowledge that morning could only bring worse.

Later his mind became floaty and confused, almost as if he were drunk, and the night seemed to break into strange, fragmented bits. It was awhile before he understood that he was actually sleeping in crazy little snatches, drifting uneasily between dark dreams and darker waking.

The voice that whispered his name was a dream voice, nothing more. He paid it no mind until it hissed his Prosperian name: "Aydin, are you here? Answer me, dammit!"

"Rowan?" He must be dreaming. There was no way this could be real, and yet the voice continued.

"Thank the gods. Where are you?"

Where are *you?* he wanted to say, but instead whispered, "I'm tied to the front of the cart."

A body slid around the edge of the cart, and a moment later a hand found him. Rowan stood before him, a dark silhouette that gripped his shoulders hard with both hands.

"Are you all right?" Rowan's hands patted him down, searching for ropes, and sawed through his hand bindings. Then he set to cutting the heavy cord around his waist.

Too late, Samik realized what would happen. "Rowan, wait. My feet first—"

The last fiber gave way, but Samik's bound feet, numb from hours of standing, could not bear his weight.

He heaved his upper body forward, trying to realign his weight, and his left calf cramped in a bolt of pain.

If he had just bent his knees and slid straight down the side of the wagon, it might still have been all right. But trying to stand had thrown him off-balance, and he fell sideways, into Rowan. Rowan, startled and trying to catch something he could hardly see, staggered back and into the donkey's harness.

The donkey's irritated bray was a death knell clamoring in their heads. Rowan fumbled at Samik's ankles, trying desperately to free him, but they both knew their chance was gone.

"God's bleeding eyes!" The guard's bellow was practically in their ears. The boys held their breaths as he hitched up over the side of the cart and peered at the donkey. He was a gray shape, not black, Samik noticed. The sun was rising. It seemed impossible he would not see them huddled practically at the donkey's feet. The guard put his head down as if ready to fall back asleep, and then, with a muttered curse, clambered out the back of the wagon. Rowan sawed frantically, sheared through the last loop, and the boys scrambled behind the wagon just as the guard's alarm cut through the dawn.

"We'll have to run for it," Rowan whispered.

Samik didn't think he *could* run, not fast enough, but he nodded grimly and they headed into the bush. They heard the shouts from the beach below, heard the scrape of a sword being pulled from its scabbard, and then Samik's guard was after them, blundering through the brush and swinging his blade before him like a scythe.

"Hurry," Rowan panted. "We have to get farther in, where it's darker." Samik could see his outline clearly now. Here by the ocean, the world would not creep slowly into daylight the way it did inland. No, soon the sun would leap over the rim of the world and blast its light across the water. He tried to make his trembling legs move faster, ignoring brambles and whipping branches, just trying to stay on his feet.

There was a roar behind him, and then Rowan cried out. A thud and another cry.

"Gotcha, you little gobshite!"

"Rowan!"

If he hadn't yelled out, maybe, just maybe, Voka wouldn't have realized he'd caught the wrong kid for a few moments longer. Maybe that would have been enough for Samik to somehow hide and then find a way to free Rowan. But he didn't really believe that. Their escape had been doomed from the minute Samik's leg betrayed him with that brutal cramp.

As it was, he yelled out just as the other two men raced up from the beach, and was pounced on almost as soon as he opened his mouth.

And now his situation was worse than before. He looked over at Rowan, clutched in the bald man's grip, and it was his dream come to life. He realized he had done exactly what he had tried not to do—dragged Rowan into danger. He was not foolish enough to hope that Jago would risk letting his friend go free. He only hoped the warlord would grant Rowan a kinder death than Samik's.

TWENTY-TWO

The sun rose in a glorious crimson ball, streaking the eastern sky with luminous trails of pink.

Rowan could hardly bear to look at it, or at Samik. They were both bruised and dirty, and Rowan was cut and bleeding across his back where the bald man had clipped him with his sword. But Samik looked so much worse than beat up. His face was the color of putty, as if his natural golden color had leached away in the night. And his eyes—his eyes were staring and wild, the eyes of someone who might start screaming and never stop.

They stood on the beach, bound hand and foot and ringed by Jago's men, and waited for the little dinghy that had been lowered from the ship to reach the shore.

"I'm sorry, Samik," Rowan muttered, and for a moment the old, haughty Aydin returned, and Rowan was glad to feel the prickle of irritation at his reply.

"What are *you* sorry about?" Like it was the stupidest thing he'd ever heard.

"I got it all wrong. I didn't have a proper plan. I…I just didn't know what to do."

But Samik was shaking his head. "No, Rowan. It is I who am sorry. I should never have got you involved in my troubles."

One of the thugs barked at them.

"He says *quiet*," Samik whispered. "Jago arrives."

JAGO LEANED HEAVILY on his attendant as he climbed out of the boat. He stumped up the beach and stood so close to the two boys that they could have reached out and touched his big belly. He gloated over his catch in silence for some time. His face, Samik saw, now pulled down at the corner of his mouth and eye on the right side. It made him look not weaker, but crazier.

"So," he said at last, his lips pulling up into a cruel, one-sided leer. "Two for the price of one. Arkan will be well fed."

Arkan. The bloodiest of Tarzine gods, the only one who accepted human sacrifice. God of revenge and deadly fire. Nobody worshipped Arkan anymore—or so he had thought. Though Samik doubted Jago truly worshipped any god; Arkan was more likely just an amusing excuse for a hideously cruel death.

Samik had already noticed the wide base of the fire that had been laid. It was as big as a bed, and that's exactly what it would be. Jago was going to burn them alive.

"Fetch the oil," said Jago. "There's plenty of room for one more. Why, they're so skinny they hardly make one man between them. And we'll need another pole for this one." He flicked a finger at Rowan.

The men looked dubiously at each other. "There's an extra oar," one ventured.

"Idiot! Does the boy look waist-high to you? Get on a horse, get into the tree zone and cut me a proper pole!"

The man was gone before Jago had closed his mouth.

With that short reprieve, Samik found his voice. From the time he had laid eyes on Jago, he had been like a ground squirrel mesmerized by the weaving asp. Now he realized there was one thing he could do.

"My lord, let my friend go, I beg you!"

Jago's big head swiveled slowly back to Samik. His eyes narrowed in displeasure.

"Did you have permission to speak?"

"Your pardon, my lord. But please, he is just a chance acquaintance. He has done nothing against your lordship. And he is just a Backender—no threat to a great warlord."

It hadn't worked. He could tell by the fury on Jago's face. The warlord's reply was the bellow of an angry bull.

"He has done nothing? The little prick tried to rob me of my prize and the justice I have sought these long months! How *dare* you call that nothing!"

Samik's head suddenly snapped to the left. He felt the stinging pain next, and only as his vision cleared did he see Ragnar inspecting a finger and then wiping its long, bloody nail on his backside. The man had struck him with such speed and precision that he hadn't seen it coming or going. He felt a hot trickle down his cheek and realized he'd been scored by the long fingernail.

That seemed to renew Jago's good spirits. He was eerily calm now as he meted out their sentence.

"No, my young friend, you will both go to Arkan. He will have you just the way he likes his offerings—screaming and very, very well cooked."

He offered Samik a lopsided parody of a tender smile and said, "It's lucky we caught you when we did. Another couple of weeks, and I would have had to give up and take your family instead."

Jago looked around irritably. "Get me some bloody shade. Am I to roast alongside these criminals?" And he stumped back to take up position beside the fire pit, where a second attendant had already set up a large, cushioned chair.

"Samik, what'd he say? What's happening?" Rowan's voice broke hoarsely as he tried to speak and then came out in a breathless squeak. Samik closed his eyes, trying to find the strength to answer. His own voice was just as strained as Rowan's, but he got the words out.

"They're going to tie us on poles and throw us on that fire. I'm so sorry, Rowan; I tried to get him to let you go, but he wouldn't."

The tears came as he choked out his next thought: "I just pray they kill us first."

ROWAN'S MIND REFUSED to let him understand what was about to happen. It simply veered away and went blank, and because of that, he submitted with apparent calm while they lashed him—legs, chest and hips—to a pole that thrust up far above his head, and watched blankly while they soaked the huge construction of logs and driftwood with oil.

But when the flames licked up hungrily, sending clouds of greasy black smoke that smelled like a kitchen accident into the air, he thought of lambs on a spit, thought, *That's what we'll smell like*, and then reality was upon him, as merciless as fire itself. The terror that he felt was a poison flooding his entire body, and when it rose up into his throat with a taste of rusty metal and a flood of spit, he retched violently and then brought up what little was left in his stomach. It dribbled over his lip and shirt, with no way to wipe it, and he didn't care. Each convulsive retch brought with it a terrible, keening wail so that he was barfing and sobbing and panting at once, and he heard Samik beside him gabbling a mix of high, panicky cries and entreaty.

Do not fear the fire.

"Ettie?" He cried her name out loud without a second thought. Ettie had been silent for so long, through the entire rescue and capture, and now..."Ettie, how can I not fear it? How can I?"

Do not fear the fire.

"What is she saying?" yelled Samik.

"She says not to fear the fire. I don't know why." Rowan could still hardly breathe, gasping out the words, but Samik immediately quieted.

"You should trust her."

The flames leaped up, and Jago waited until the oil had burned off and the structure was a waist-high, hungry bed of fire. Then he made a lazy motion with one hand.

"Put them in."

The men tipped the boys backward so they could slide the poles down through the ropes to make handles at either end and hoist them up. Then they froze in shock as a huge gray shape streaked silently down the slope, hurtled past them and leaped at Jago's throat.

"K'waaf!" The words burst out of Samik's throat in a ragged, sobbing cheer. Brave heart, and true.

Jago went down with a shriek, chair and all, struggling ineffectually to fend off the great dog. K'waaf sank his teeth deep and shook his huge head back and forth, tearing out Jago's life. His growls filled Samik's head, even after the men dropped him facedown on the ground and raced to defend their boss.

And then he heard the piercing yelps of an injured dog, and even as he cried out, "No! K'waaf, oh, no!" the great dog fell silent.

He could not bear to look, but he had to. He turned his head and saw the men sheathing their swords and clustering around Jago. K'waaf lay still, his fur soaked in blood, more staining the sand beneath him. He looked at Samik and thumped his tail once, feebly. Then his eyes closed.

Samik turned his face into the sand and wept for the friend who had given his life to protect them. K'waaf had killed Jago, he was all but certain. But there were still five men who would take their revenge, and a shipful more. Too much for one dog, however great of heart.

Then Rowan spoke to him, and his voice was so out of place on that hellish beach that it pulled Samik out of his grief. Rowan's voice was full of wonder.

"Samik, look!"

TWENTY-THREE

Rowan didn't notice her at first, his attention fixed on Wolf. Neither did Jago's men. But then one of them faltered, staring at the fire. Soon they were all aghast, staring with the same wide eyes and open mouths.

From the pyre's depth, a great light was growing—not the dancing orange tongues of the fire, but white and steady and incredibly bright, like the very heart of the sun. Rising in that white light, a form was taking shape.

And now, oh now, he could see her. The round blue eyes, the honey-blond braids. The sweet, plain, winsome face. She gazed at him, and smiled—smiled! And as the flames licked around her, she grew first more vivid, and then larger, until she loomed over Jago's men like a round-eyed, braided djinn, dangerous and powerful beyond all imagination.

Any who still held swords let them fall from nerveless hands. Some knelt with their heads to the sand.

Ettie's smile vanished. Her mouth opened and red flame shot out. The blue eyes became burning coals. Flames licked down her braids and eyebrows and streamed from her fingers. The amethyst around her neck glowed red. She drew herself up and then *rushed* at the warlord's men.

They scattered before her like chickens before a fox. Falling over themselves, and each other, to get to the boat, they shoved and fought like players in a comic pantomime to get it launched and everyone in.

Then they were gone, and Ettie was once more a normal-sized girl with plump cheeks and a sweet smile, shimmering deep within the light.

She smiled tenderly at Rowan once more—his vision blurred from the tears that swam in his eyes, and he blinked furiously to bring her back into focus. *I see you, Ettie! Finally, I see you.*

One last thing.

She drifted over to Wolf where he lay bleeding. His tail twitched as she approached, but wagging it was beyond him now. And she laid herself over him like a blanket, and while Rowan watched in wonder, the white light grew brighter and bigger, until he could no longer see her form, and Wolf appeared to be bathed in a cloud of brilliant light.

Then she rose. She was faint now, her blue eyes still blue but her features growing mistier by the second. She was going for good, Rowan knew. He would not look on her face or hear her voice again.

Her hand drifted to the amethyst over her heart. And then she raised her hand and opened and closed her fist at him, a gesture that both broke his heart and filled it with love. It was how Ettie had waved "bye-bye" when she was just a baby, opening and closing her hand instead of waving her arm. Rowan had thought it so cute and funny that, when she grew out of it, he taught her to keep doing it as their own special wave. If Ettie had lived, he thought, they would still be waving to each other that way in their old age.

Stay! he wanted to plead. But he knew he mustn't. He didn't want her to become one of the unhappy, lost souls that Samik had described. It was time for her to go.

Rowan couldn't raise his bound arms, but he opened and closed his hand all the same. He knew she could see it.

"Bye-bye, Ettie," he whispered. She was fading, disappearing into the light. That golden light floated over and enveloped him, filling him with the most wondrous feeling of peace and comfort, and then it winked out, and she was gone.

There was no blinking back the tears now; they filled his eyes and spilled down his cheeks, and he didn't even try to hold them back.

WRAPPED UP IN HIS OWN complicated, painful mixture of grief, gratitude and even joy, Rowan did not hear Samik's giddy laughter. But he could not ignore the rough tongue slobbering over the back of his neck, or the powerful blast of dog breath that came with it. It was Wolf—bloody, limping, but not dead, not even close to dead. *Thank you, Ettie.* Rowan flung his arms around the dog's neck and buried his face in his rough fur, and that was when he realized his hands were free. In fact, all of him was free—his ropes lay unknotted on the ground, beside the hateful pole.

He looked then to Samik, who was sitting up, rubbing his wrists.

"Samik—did you see?"

Samik nodded solemnly, speechless for once. And then Rowan was crying again, sure that Samik would have something caustic to say about it, but unable to hold it back. But Samik didn't say a word. He scooted over beside Rowan and wrapped his arms around him and held him tight until his breath began to steady. Then he spoke very quietly in his ear: "Your sister is a beautiful soul. She will be happy now. And you must find a way to be happy, too, for her sake. It is what she wants for you."

Rowan nodded into Samik's shoulder. Then he sat up, scrubbed at his eyes and sighed.

He sniffed. "You smell bad."

"Yes," Samik agreed cheerfully. "As do you."

"I puked on my shirt. What did you do?"

"Crapped myself." Samik carefully pulled off his boot, reached into the hidden pocket and pulled out a small knife.

He wiped it carefully on a leaf, and then flashed Rowan one of his trademark grins. "All the way down to my boots."

BOTH BOYS FELT DREAMY and reluctant to move. Rowan just wanted to hold that moment when he floated in Ettie's light as long as he possibly could. But they both knew they couldn't stay.

It was Samik who broached it. "Rowan, we have to get out of here. I doubt the ones who captured us will ever set foot on this beach again. But the others, the ones who didn't see—they might come for Jago's body." He gestured toward the dead warlord, and Rowan unwillingly flicked his eyes the same way. He had managed to forget about Jago, but now the savaged carcass crowded out his lovely memory of Ettie. The warlord's neck was crusted and black where K'waaf had torn it open, the sand beneath him stained.

"And they'd better not find us here," Samik concluded. He pulled himself stiffly to his feet and brushed off the sand.

Rowan nodded and slowly rose. Gods, he was exhausted. Now he felt how long he'd been up, how long since he'd eaten, the toll that fear and fatigue and overwhelming love had taken on him. He walked like an old man, trudging his slow way through the sand to the higher, firmer ground where he had first found Samik.

They considered—and decided against—taking the horses. Better not to give Jago's men any reason to continue the pursuit. Instead, they made their way to where poor Daisy and Dusty waited, and then they hoisted K'waaf into the wagon, where he eased himself onto the floor and promptly fell asleep.

"Wish we could do the same," said Samik. Rowan nodded, watering the mules briefly and giving them each an apologetic nose rub. They were like old friends now, these mules, and he knew he was pushing them too hard. "A proper stable when we get there, girls," he murmured.

Luckily, they didn't have to go far until the land opened up and they could turn around. The two boys climbed onto the front bench and looked at each other.

"Stormy Head or Kingstown?"

Rowan considered. Ward and Cardinal's place was much too far. Kingstown, he guessed, was a bit farther than Stormy Head—but there were friends there, and free lodging. They needed sleep and food and a bath, and K'waaf needed doctoring. Rowan flexed his shoulder blades experimentally. The cut on his back stung and ached at the same time, but he didn't think it was too bad.

"Kingstown. Let's go, girls." He shook the reins gently— too gently for any self-respecting mule to respond to. But as if they knew that relief would only come from getting somewhere civilized, the mules headed out with their patient, dogged pace.

"If I fall asleep, poke me," he said. He hoped he could find the address Marten had given him without trouble.

He wondered who would give directions to two stinking, filthy, bloodstained travelers.

ROWAN'S HEAD SNAPPED UP—again—and this time opening his eyes was a physical struggle. It was no good; he would have to pull over and just pray they were not pursued. Samik was already asleep, bent over with his head on his knees despite the jouncing of the cart.

The drama of the night before had left them with a buzzy, high-strung energy that had carried Rowan through the first hour or two on the road. He had replayed all that had happened over and over in his mind, especially the beautiful feeling when Ettie had hovered over him. After coming so close to a terrible death, the very fact of being alive gave a glow to the world.

And then the euphoric feeling drained away, and the midmorning sun grew hot and beat down on his head and shoulders. The need for sleep became a tidal pull that sucked him deeper with each wave.

He was watching for a good place to pull off the road when he saw a man trudging ahead of them. He was heavily burdened, with a bulging pack on his back and dragging some kind of big sack along the ground.

As the mules slowly overtook him, Rowan gave the man a quick appraisal. The walker was an older man, plainly dressed but not impoverished-looking, and his face,

Rowan decided, based on nothing but his own hunch, looked honest. He pulled the girls to a halt.

"Going to Kingstown?" Rowan asked.

"Aye." The man looked up hopefully, but his face went still as he took in the state of the two boys. Samik, lifting his head up in bleary confusion, offered a wan grin.

"We had a rough night."

A slow nod. "Right enough." He considered awhile, then his shoulders twitched in a brief shrug, and he asked Rowan, "Can you give a lift?"

"Do you know how to drive a mule team?"

The man nodded. "Surely."

"Then, yes, if you can drive us to Kingstown and take us to this address." Rowan rummaged in the pouch under his shirt, pulled out a crumpled scrap of parchment and handed it over.

The man didn't take the paper. "What's it say? I don't read." Rowan's hopes fell a little, but as he recited the address, the man's face pulled into a grin of recognition.

"Why, Sumach Lane ain't but three or four blocks from where I'm headed! I'll take ye right to the door."

Five minutes later, Rowan and Samik were stretched out on their bunks, moaning in gratitude. And then they were gone.

TWENTY-FOUR

Samik woke with a start, realized the caravan had stopped moving and tried to sit up. Pain shot through his body.

"Muki save me." The words came out in a long groan.

Rowan snapped awake. "What?" He looked wide-eyed and jumpy, like a rabbit ready to bolt.

"Everything hurts," said Samik. "Everything. Plus, I think we have arrived."

Sure enough, a second later the canvas flap parted and their driver's head poked in.

"Here we are, lads. Sumach Lane, like you asked. I'll be taking my leave now."

Rowan got slowly to his feet and went out the caravan door. Samik wanted nothing more than to put his head down and go back to sleep—the need for it was like a deep, yawning hunger. But then he heard the bang of a door, a shriek, a girl's voice exclaiming and gabbling and then more voices, men's voices.

The caravan door screeched.

"Mother of all, look at you!"

Shay. Samik opened one eye, confirmed that Shay was, indeed, kneeling by his bunk, and tore himself away from the sweet arms of sleep.

"Oh, my poor boy, what on earth have you been up to?" Shay leaned in as if to smooth back his hair or touch his cheek, and her nose wrinkled.

"Rowan and I are both beyond filthy, I'm afraid." With a sigh, Samik braced himself for the pain to come and struggled to a sit.

Shay's eyes widened at his grimace. "You're really hurt."

"Walking will be even better. Give me your arm, will you, if you can bear the smell?"

Samik's legs felt like he'd run a hundred miles, but by the time he hobbled to the door, they had loosened up enough to let him manage the steps. Outside, Rowan was surrounded by his concerned band members. Shay waded in.

"Lads, lads, give the poor boy room so he can get inside. Can't you see these two are dead on their feet?" She came back to Samik. "Need an arm in, or can you manage?"

"I can do it." He was grateful all the same when she led them into a cozy room and let him sink into a deep chair.

"Now, then." Shay stood in front of them, clearly in charge. "We're all dying to know what happened, but I won't be able to listen properly until we get you cleaned up and taken care of. So I'm going to go put on a huge kettle of water, and I will personally kill you both if you tell this lot"—she waved at the men who were now standing around in the parlor—"one word before I return!"

"Do you need doctoring, lads?" Marten looked with concern at the bloodstains on the back of Rowan's shirt.

Rowan shook his head. "I think I'm all right. I might get you to take a look when I'm in the bath, but it's not bleeding anymore." He met Samik's eye. "Samik, how about you?"

Samik considered. His face was swollen where it had been hit, and his skin was raw in places where the ropes had sawed in. He was bruised from being rattled around in the wagon too, but mostly he was just incredibly sore from that long night on his feet. But—"K'waaf!" he exclaimed. "Where is he?"

Marten disappeared. Samik heard the screech of the caravan door, and then K'waaf was at his side, his big tail whipping back and forth so hard that one of the men took a hasty step out of its way.

Samik bent forward—demon's breath, that hurt—and carefully, gently checked the big dog's coat. Then he had K'waaf lie down and present his belly, and he methodically examined his underside. The fur was stiff and stained in places with blood, but Samik was relieved to find the actual injuries were all scabbed over. Incredible. His eyes filled with tears as he remembered how K'waaf had lain on the beach, his life soaking into the sand. *Thank you, Ettie, lovely soul.*

He straightened to find Rowan's eyes fixed on him, full of concern, and smiled through the tears.

"He'll be fine." He shook his head in wonder, and Rowan smiled, understanding all that couldn't be said. The chatter of the room faded away, and Samik knew they were both remembering that beautiful moment when Ettie's light lay over them like a blessing.

Shay reappeared. "Are you hungry, you two?"

Samik's stomach roared into life. He was starved—how could he not have noticed?

ROWAN AND SAMIK were both writing letters.

Samik's was easy:

I am in the capital city of Kingstown, and will finally have a chance to send you this letter that I have been carrying about for weeks. Now I can add on the most important news: Jago is dead. K'waaf killed him, but I do not think there will be any reprisals, not unless Jago's followers are so loyal they dare to brave the wrath of the divine! I will tell you the whole story when I see you. As soon as I can earn my passage, I am coming home.

I pray you are all well,
Samik

Rowan's letter was much harder. He was writing to Ward and Cardinal. He'd only lost a few days from his "detour" to find Samik, but getting back on the road again was more than he could manage. He'd had enough of traveling alone—if that was cowardly, so be it. He hoped to find a textile merchant or carpet dealer who did business with his aunt and uncle and leave the letter to send back on the next delivery wagon.

He wrote about the death of his family, and then stopped. Should he tell them what had just happened? The thought of writing out the whole complicated story of Jago and Samik was daunting, and, in any case, it just felt wrong to tack it on to a death notice. His Aunt Cardinal was quick to laugh and cry, and he knew she would be sobbing as she read his account. She was very fond of Ettie, he remembered, and felt a quick stab of regret at missing his visit.

In the end, he settled on reassuring them that he had found a good position and giving them the address of Marten's tall, narrow house in Kingstown. Once he had settled in with his new band, he wrote, he hoped to be able to take some time off to visit—perhaps in the fall. Meantime, if business ever brought either of them to Kingstown, he hoped they would look him up.

He signed his name laboriously—*Your loving nephew, Rowan*—and thought with envy of Samik's quick, elegant script. Samik had pulled out a couple of crumpled pages covered in even, beautiful handwriting, dashed off another half-page in what seemed like the blink of an eye, and had the whole thing addressed and ready to send while Rowan was still thinking. He'd always been better at writing out music than words.

With a sigh, he wrote Ward's address on the back of the page, rolled up the parchment so the address showed, then tied and sealed it. Then he set out to see if he could follow Marten's directions to the merchant district and find someone who knew his uncle.

IT TOOK ROWAN MOST of the afternoon to find the textile district and work his way through the various merchants until he found a solid option.

"Oh, indeed, I know your uncle well," the round little man had said. "A fine business, quality goods. I'm expecting a delivery any day, in fact." He had been glad to take Rowan's message and promised to send it back with the delivery driver.

It was a relief to have that long-overdue duty discharged. Rowan made the long walk back briskly, more sure of his way now, and got home in time for dinner. The dark city house didn't feel like a true home, not yet—but it was comfortable and congenial, and Rowan even liked that Marten had assigned a work schedule, ensuring that the everyday tasks like marketing, cooking and cleanup were organized and shared. He had been a bit worried that the household might be grimy and chaotic, everyone fending for himself while the bigger tasks were ignored. But Marten was having none of that. "This house is my nest egg," he had explained, "and I aim to keep my investment sound."

Samik sauntered in just as they were sitting down. "How'd you make out?" Rowan asked. With a grin, Samik pulled two large silver coins out of his pocket and clinked them together. Rowan's eyes widened.

"Are those double dallions? Where'd you get them?"

"At the docks. I believe I've just found a way to earn my passage home."

One of the harbormasters had overheard Samik speaking to the captain of a Tarzine ship. Noticing his Prosperian clothing, he called Samik over.

"Here, lad. Do you also speak Prosperian?"

Samik was promptly enlisted to translate for the harbor-master as he registered and assessed the docking fees for a Tarzine ship that had just made port. "The captain and first mate speak about five words of our language between them, far as I can tell," the harbormaster grumbled. "Don't know what they expect to accomplish here in that Tarzine jibber-jabber."

The ship's captain, whose own interpreter was stricken with fever, was relieved to meet Samik and hired him on the spot. He had spent the afternoon helping with the delivery of one cargo and negotiating the sale of the trade goods the captain had brought on his own. "And then we shared a very nice bottle of wine," Samik concluded. "The first I have had in a good long time."

Kingstown was the preferred port of call for Tarzine trade ships, and the harbor was always busy through the mild season. Samik figured that between busking for the Tarzine sailors and translating, he could make good coin at the docks. He had accepted Marten's offer to put down a bedroll in the sitting room, but drew the line when Shay enlisted the others to cover his share of the food.

"Sleeping on your floor is one thing. Taking money out of your pockets is quite another. I am enough in your debt already."

THE BOYS BEGAN TO SETTLE INTO a new routine. Rowan's days were busy with rehearsing, performing, taking his turn at the housework, exploring his new city. Samik was often at the docks, working hard to get himself home. Before they knew it, a half-moon had gone by.

Soon the band would be on the road again, doing the circuit of summer festivals and fairs, but for now Rowan was happy to put down some tentative roots. Shay often went with him as he walked the city, pointing out the sights and filling him in on the gossip that constantly swirls around a royal seat. And he and Samik were getting along really well. Of course, they were no longer living in each other's pocket, and that made things easier. But Rowan didn't think that was the whole story. Something had changed between them, that day on the beach. He tried not to think about how soon Samik would be gone for good.

It was his day to cook dinner, and he was at the market with a lengthy list. Shopping for six people was a lot different from the meager purchases he had made when it was just himself. He had two heavy baskets laden, and was considering whether there was enough money left over to splurge on a mess of new-harvest mushrooms, when Wolf burst out in a volley of ferocious barking and plunged into the crowd. The leash ripped out of Rowan's hand, pulling a basket with it.

"Wolf, no! Come!" It was futile—the big dog couldn't even hear him above his own frantic barks. Not knowing what else to do, and fearing Wolf was about to attack some innocent marketer, Rowan pelted after him. Too late another thought came—that Jago's men had followed them, and Wolf had caught their scent.

It was neither. As he pushed through the last people blocking his way, Rowan stopped in astonishment.

Wolf was on his hind legs, his great paws draped over the shoulders of a small, dark, pear-shaped man in elegant but outlandish—and unmistakably Tarzine—clothing. The man was rubbing the dog's wiry gray belly as Wolf drooled down his back.

Rowan walked slowly up to them. The man caught his eye and, with a short Tarzine command, dropped Wolf into a sit, though his long tail continued to wag furiously.

He looked nothing like Samik, until he smiled. Rowan took a deep breath, summoned up one of his few words of Tarzine and stuck out his hand.

"*Siko*. You must be Samik's father."

"THEN IF YOU WILL SIGN HERE, everything is in order." Samik pointed out the spot, and the harbormaster passed a quill over to the ship's captain. "Welcome to Prosper," he added, though the harbormaster had said no such thing. They had no sense of ceremony, these Prosperians.

A volley of barking caught his attention, and he looked up to see the last thing he would ever have expected: Rowan sauntering down the long wharf with Samik's father in tow. Alerted by K'waaf's barking, Rowan stopped and scanned the crowd, then pointed Samik out to Ziv.

But Samik was running by then, his long legs flying over the uneven boards of the quay. He landed against his father so hard that he nearly bowled him over.

AND SO THEIR GOODBYE CAME SOONER than either of them had expected. Rowan stood by the carriage that would take Samik and Ziv to the docks, dismayed to find himself close to tears. Samik had become his family at a time when he was utterly alone, he realized. Now he was losing his family again.

"Well, my Backender friend." Samik regarded Rowan steadily. "It's barely two moons since we first met."

Gods, it seemed a lifetime ago.

Samik stepped up and put his hands on Rowan's shoulders. "We are brothers now," he said. "And I will want to know how you are faring. So keep that address I gave you, and send me a message now and again, yes?"

Rowan nodded, not trusting himself to speak. And then Samik moved closer.

Will he kiss me again? Rowan braced himself. He hadn't changed his expression, he could swear it, but Samik gave an amused hoot of laughter.

"No, don't worry, there'll be none of that." They hugged each other, and Rowan held on tight. He heard Samik's voice murmur in his ear, "In any case, I'd say it's Shay you'd like to be kissing, yes? I wish you luck."

And then Samik was swallowed up by the carriage, and the carriage clattered down the street and was gone.

ROWAN STOOD ON THE LITTLE FRONT stoop for a long time, thinking about all that had happened, wondering if he and Samik would ever cross paths again. It could happen, he supposed. It wouldn't surprise him if Samik actually pursued his scheme to bring "decent wine" to Prosper.

The door opened, and Shay stuck her head out. "Are you coming in for dinner? River has made some kind of pasty. It smells like it might be edible."

"In a minute." Rowan wasn't quite ready for the warmth and good-natured ribbing of the dinner table.

Shay came out and stood silently beside him on the weathered boards.

"You'll miss him," she said at last. She had slipped her hand into his, Rowan noticed. It felt nice.

"I will." And Hazel and Cashel and Ettie, the great losses that loomed over every smaller one. He would miss them, always.

And yet...he could also enjoy Shay's hand in his and hope it meant more than friendly sympathy. He could look forward to dinner, and feel excited about the new tune he was learning. That loss and laughter could co-exist so comfortably—it was a mystery as baffling as any ghost.

He had to work at the smile, but it came. "Right. Let's go try our luck with River's cooking."

EPILOGUE

The heavy crate arrived addressed to Rowan, with a note from Samik.

Rowan Redwing,

My family and I send this crate as a small, utterly inadequate thank-you for all you did for me—from taking me in, to saving my life. It is very good wine, and I charge you to have a most excellent party with your friends on Sumach Lane with it. Savor it slowly with a good meal, and then get blind drunk and dance through the house together. The remaining bottles (if any!) you may drink as you wish.

This next part is just for you: it is a song, the first I have ever written, and in Prosperian, no less! It is about you when we first met.

My heart goes out to you
Poor weary traveler
Forced to travel this world alone
Forced to wander away from home

You must sow what you cannot reap
You must hold what you cannot keep
You must fear what you cannot know
You must feel what you cannot speak

You can't see the angels
Gathered all around you
You must lie in the cold clay
You must travel to the end of the day.

I would never share this with you if I thought you were still this person, but you are not. I hope you can read this and see how far you have come in one short season. You have come home.
Now go drink up!
Samik
P.S. I hope you have kissed the lovely Shay by now. If not, perhaps you should hold back one bottle to share just with her. Courage, man!

Rowan looked at the song for a long time. There seemed no end to Samik's ability to surprise, even from the other end of the island. A part of him winced to think his friend had seen him in this light. The other part, the greater part, was almost overcome by how perfectly Samik had captured how Rowan's life had felt back then—even, somehow, in the parts that didn't really make sense. And Samik was right; he didn't feel this way anymore.

On the back of the page, Samik had written out the tune. Rowan fetched his button box, sat it on his knee and began to play.

ACKNOWLEDGMENTS

It gets repetitive, thanking the same people in each novel, but it's really important to recognize that there is a whole team behind every single book, and most don't even get their names on the copyright page. So, I am very grateful to all the people who helped make this book a reality, including:

- My agent, Lynn Bennett, of Transatlantic Literary Agency. If you hadn't been generous enough to read that very first manuscript and find it a home, I'm not sure any of the others would have followed.
- My smart, talented and patient editor, Sarah Harvey. It has got to be a challenge to work with a writer who is also an opinionated know-it-all editor! But because I'm an editor, I am deeply aware of how valuable your work is. *Redwing* is a much better book because of you.
- To all the staff at Orca, from publisher to publicist, designer to copyeditor.
- Finally, my thanks to the wonderful Irish songwriter John Spillane, who generously gave permission for me to abridge his song, "Poor Weary Wanderer," and call it Samik's.

Holly Bennett is the author of *Shapeshifter*, *The Warrior's Daughter* and the Bonemender series, all published by Orca. She is also a freelance editor and writer working from her home office in Peterborough, Ontario. Her husband and three sons are all musical, so it seemed inevitable that she would eventually write a book about a boy musician.